The Traveler's League: The Pirates of Skuggi

Written by Nick Goss
Cover Design: TS95 Studios
Illustrations: RaeAnna Goss
Editor: SJS Editorial Services
Special thanks to Michelle Chadd

Published by Nicholas Goss, Nashville, TN

Printed in the United States of America
ISBN 978-1-7904164-0-0 (Paperback)

Dedication

For my wife.

The Pirates of Skuggi

Book 4 of the Traveler's League

By Nick Goss

Table of Contents

The Trollhammer

Prologue

The coast of Hapis finally disappeared behind them. The longship had opened her two big triangular sails only two hours ago. When they departed the night before, the wind had been against them and they had to *row* the ship out into the ocean in the dark of night, with no lanterns. It was back breaking work to get the ship into the trade winds this time of year.

The sun had just come up before them. And the thin strip of land they had departed from was visible only for a couple of hours before vanishing beneath the horizon. Now that they were out of sight of the Marsh Troll watchtowers along the coast, they could raise their sails and let the winds take them across the sea to Sirihbaz.

They were on a secret mission. The rebel Queen Diambi had ordered that the *Trollhammer* be used to transport a very important passenger to her ally the Crystal Queen at once. This passenger was a prisoner, bound and gagged, and tied to the foot of the foremast. The prisoner was a young man who was caught trespassing in the forests of Hapis, dangerously close to Diambi's secret encampment. When her soldiers had seized this young man, she ordered a sack be pulled over his head and not removed until he was safely imprisoned in Castle Mavros under the Crystal Queen's guard.

The sailors who had rowed in silence all night, now rested along the sides of the vessel. They muttered and murmured to each other, whispering angrily while leering at the prisoner in the front of the ship.

The *Trollhammer* was a 'longboat.' It was at least fifty feet long, and about ten feet wide in the middle. Both ends of the ship tapered together, allowing it to be rowed in either direction. But the front of the ship had a wooden figurehead that was carved into the shape of a vicious looking hammer, and the keel that ran from the figure head, and along the bottom of the ship to its rudder was made out of solid iron. The ship had eight oars on each side, each manned by two sailors. This ship could reach great speeds and was designed to ram its enemies. But out in the open ocean, there was no need to row. From each of its two masts hung a huge forest green sail in the shape of a tilted triangle. When the wind caught the sails, the ship was pulled gracefully through the water and slipped through and over the sea swells with ease.

Atop the mainmast, the mast towards the back of the ship, sat a crow's nest: a small wooden platform at the very top, where a sailor kept constant watch for land, danger, and weather.

Now, more than ever it was important to scan the horizon towards their home shores of Hapis to ensure they weren't being followed, or that the Marsh Trolls hadn't spotted them and started signalling other towers farther down the coast. The Marsh Trolls ships were slower than the *Trollhammer*, but the chain of signalling towers along the coast allowed them to spot and intercept enemy vessels with ease.

The watchman strained his eyes for hours and saw no signs of danger towards the coast. But when he turned his gaze towards the great sea ahead of them, he saw a tiny gray dot on the horizon.

"Ship ahoy!" he shouted to the captain below.

The captain jumped to his feet and looked through his looking glass - a clear piece of crystal lodged in one end of a leather tube. Through the looking glass he saw a ship. She was a broad, wooden cargo ship with two sets of square sails on both of its masts. The sails were ripped and tattered. It appeared that the winds had ripped the sheets free and that the crew had no way to control it.

It was a vessel in distress, and the code of courtesy demanded that the *Trollhammer* aid them.

Within half an hour they were in shouting distance of the poor cargo vessel.

Captain Thorne ordered his sailors to pull in the sails and prepare to come alongside under oars. They approached the rear of the cargo ship and came along her starboard (right) side. As they did, the captain looked at the stained glass windows of the cargo ships Captain's cabin. He was instantly jealous. If only Hapis had the power to once again build such great ships then he could command a large navy of ships and have his own Captains quarters. For now he had to settle with open decked row boats.

As they come alongside, Captain Thorne called out in a loud voice,

"Ahoy there!.. I'm Captain Thorne of Diambi's Hapis Navy. We've come to assist... anyone there?"

There was a still quiet. No one called back from the cargo ship. No one could be seen running about the decks or crawling in the rigging.

"Hello?" Thorne yelled again. But there didn't seem to be anyone aboard the big wooden ship to answer.

"I think this ship has been abandoned, Cap'n" said one of the sailors.

Thorne thought that it might be a good idea to board the cargo ship and see if it truly was abandoned, and if so, if there may be any useful provisions they could secure for their trip.

I wonder if we could get this old ship in working order again? I could take that Captain's cabin for myself and my sailors would have a place to escape the weather in rough seas...

Thorne turned to his sailors and said, "Secure the *Trollhammer* to the side of the ship. We're going to board her."

Two sailors, one at the front of the *Trollhammer* and one at the rear, tossed grappling hooks over the sides of the cargo ship and secured the ropes with big tight knots. The two ships were tied together.

Just then a rope ladder tumbled down the side of the cargo ship and dangled in front of Thorne. He glanced up and and was stunned to see a small, manish figure standing on the cargo ship's deck looking down at him. The man was about three feet tall and had a roundish shape. A white beard covered most of his face and his skin was pale as the moon. His clothes were bleached to a dirty white and ripped at all the edges.

It was a Wollipog.

"Ahoy there!" Thorne called up, "We'd like permission to come aboard, dwarf."

But the Wollipog said nothing. He stood as still as a statue and looked down at them. He had a look of terror in his eyes.

"I said we'd like to board, with your permission... Answer me, dwarf! Do you need assistance? Can we board?"

Thorne noticed that the dwarf couldn't answer, because a white cloth had been tied around his mouth. He was gagged and unable to answer.

"Permission granted Captain" called a young boy's voice from somewhere on the ship.

All at once, a two dozen faces appeared over the railing above. They were all boys' faces, dirty mean faces, with strange hats, and bright smudges of war paint in various designs. Each boy held a crossbow, cocked and loaded with iron bolts. And they aimed directly at the heads of the *Trollhammer's* sailors.

Captain Thorne was furious at the bad behavior of these boys. "I ought to take you over my knee and teach you a lesson, you little brats.... who's in charge here?!" he shouted.

"I am" a boy called from the back of the big ship. Thorne looked up and to his left. Standing on the poop deck (the deck above the Captain's cabin where they steer the ship) stood a boy no older than eleven or twelve. He had piercing blue eyes and a face covered in freckles. His snotty little nose pointed up giving him the look of a spoiled little trouble making brat. Upon his head he wore the strangest hat Thorne had ever seen; the pelt of a tiger's head that draped down over the boy's ears.

"Tiger Master, at your service." The boy gave an elaborate bow. "And you, Captain Thorne, are my prisoner."

"I'll die before I surrender to some brat child." Thorne growled. "Now put those toys away before you hurt yourselves."

Tiger Master put a hand to his mouth and shouted towards his crew, "Colors!"

A tall, skinny boy with a face covered with pimples began to furiously pull a rope through a pulley and up, up, up, raised an enormous black flag.

The flag was as dark as night in a cave, with the skull and crossbones in bright white stretching across it.

Tiger Master proudly saluted the flag, then turned to Thorne. "You are now the prisoners of the Pirates of Skuggi. You will be taken aboard our ship, where your fates will be determined by my crew according to the laws of piracy and the pleasure of Old Duppy. If you do not surrender peacefully, we will kill everyone one of you and burn your ship to ash.... You have only a moment to decide Captain Thorne... Do you surrender?"

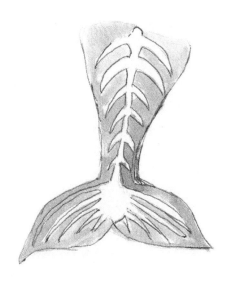

Albion's Curse

The sweltering heat of the jungle awoke the boy from a gloomy dream. The thick canopy above blocked most of the newly risen sun's light. But the stifling humidity thickened and the animal stink signaled that it was time to get out of bed and face another cursed day on the Island of Isango.

Albion flopped his legs over the sides of his hammock and checked the ground a few feet below. The last time he jumped out without looking, he narrowly escaped the sting of a scorpion's' tale. That may have been yesterday. Or maybe it was a week ago. Or a month. Everyday was the same. Every day was a curse.

The ground below was clear of stinging critters and sharp pointed obstacles. The boy jumped down, crouched for a moment, and listened carefully. He was mindful to be still after making noise in this place. Many times before he had irritated a great beast nearby. It was an ugly beast with vicious black claws, and two horns that protruded from a great head that looked somewhat like a crocodile's. It had leathery orange skin and a long horse-like neck. Most of all, it had a short temper and an absolute intolerance for anything intruding on its jungle territory.

After a moment of perfectly motionless silence, Albion knew it was safe to start moving. The edge of the jungle was only a few yards down the path and he softly, yet quickly, padded his way to it. The jungle path ended as it spilled out onto the beach. Pushing the wall of giant palm leaves and branches out of his way, Albion placed his feet in the dry yellow sand. It was still cool from a full night's worth of ocean breezes. That was the only thing about this place that was pleasant. The wind that blew in off the ocean carried the salty smell of fish and crustaceans. Seaweed and kelp beds from beyond faraway reefs peppered their scent into the tumbles of wind that brushed the shores before breaking on the hard green foliage of the jungle canopy.

The wind carried the smell of Albion's memories and affections. It caressed his face and ran its cool tendrils through his tangled dirty blonde hair. Every windy gust to rush by his ears seemed to whisper *come home, Son of the sea.*

The waves that rushed in before the wind were small and rythmic. Their crashes spread thin and fanned out and up the beach before retracting, then sliding under the next tumbling wave. The crashing, fizzing, and settling water also called to Albion. *Come home. Your home. Come home, Albion. Son of the sea. Come home. We miss you.*

Albion wanted nothing more than to come home. He wanted nothing more than to break the curse, and return home. But he was banished. He was cursed. It was impossible to force his way back. But something inside him pressed him closer to the water. His feet, cracked and dry, crushed into the sand, one after the other. Step by step he got closer and closer to the small sweeping, tumbling waves as they rolled up the beach, and back into ocean.

He knew that today would be no different than any other day, but he couldn't help himself. He had to try *one more time.*

Finally he reached the glossy wet sand that had just been washed by the sheet of bubbling fizzing sea water. He stepped towards the water and waited for the next wave to run up to him. Maybe, just *maybe,* this time the water would blurble between his toes and over his feet, refreshing them before washing up his shins and over his knees.

The water rolled in and he walked out to meet it.

The approaching line of the water split in two and rolled around both of his feet, then rejoined behind him. The sand under his feet did not give way as the water rushed back down the beach either. The spot on which he stood was completely dry.

Albion, more angry than sad, stomped into the surf. The water was knee deep, but did not touch his knees. From his waist down he was surrounded by dry air. The sand at his feet, normally awash with two feet of salt water was bone dry.

Furious, Albion plunged forward reaching out his arms to swim, to grab any part of the ocean. But the ocean evaded him, and he fell on his face on dry sand. He scraped his knee on the sharp remains of a broken sand dollar, also dried to a crisp by the curse that surrounded Albion.

He stood up, now more than ten feet under the surface of the water. The light streaming through the waves above cast glistening blue streamers all about him. He could see schools of small fish darting back and forth with the waves, gulping up whatever was driven out of the retreating sand and wash.

But Albion was dry. He was surrounded three feet in every direction by air. He was encased in a dry bubble that allowed no water near him.

It was his curse.

As he walked back up the slope towards the beach, a school of fish rushed by and one fish was unlucky enough to penetrate Albion's boundary of air. It was moving quickly and struck him in the calf. He reached down to grab his little friend and throw him back to the water outside his arid sphere. But when he touched it, there was a quiver of pain, and a sharp twist of the fish's tail. The gills stopped pumping and the fish instantly died.

Albion returned to the beach and spent the entire day staring out over the ocean, smelling the salty sea, embracing the wind's airy strokes of empathy, and wishing beyond hope that one day he could return home.

That night, as the sun sank below the ocean's horizon, and the two crescent moons rose, Albion lay in his hammock in the jungle. His heart was broken. He was broken. He was angry and sorry. A single tear slipped from his eye, and then vanished before it found his cheek. Not even in sorrow and grief was he allowed to feel the moisture of a single watery drop.

As he drifted off to sleep, his last words for that day, like every day before, drifted up through the jungle canopy to be carried by the winds and out to sea...

"I'm sorry, Father. Please..."

Shadow Bay

Reuben sat on the dry desert floor staring at the strange fire. It was the only thing in the dark three o'clock world that gave any light. Dusty pebbles and small dead wood sticks lay here and there but no living plants were anywhere to be found. There was no life of any kind. The fire was the only thing that seemed alive... and the cave.

The gaping hole in the foot of the monstrous rock cliff in front of Reuben looked like the mouth of some rock monster begging to be fed. Reuben had arrived in this world somewhere back in the throat of that cave. When he activated the magic of the timepiece he had been in his backyard treehouse. The sun was shining and robins were garbling. It was a perfect Saturday afternoon and Reuben spent the day *whooshing* back and forth from the two o'clock world. He had lost his reflection and spent hours trying to figure out how to restore it. But something changed the last time he rubbed the timepiece's faded lid. The pocket watch set itself to three o'clock, forcing him into a world of night and shadow.

He was terrified when he opened his eyes over and over again but could see nothing but the deepest, most complete darkness he ever could have imagined. But after a few minutes his eyes adjusted and the faint red glow of the fire, just outside the cave's entrance, washed over a corner wall and Reuben was able to find his way out.

He had no idea who had started the fire, and was curious as to why it never seemed to die out. The sticks he had thrown into the fire hours ago, were wrapped in red flame, but never charred or dwindled. They just kept burning.

He walked all along the canyon wall but found no way to climb to the top. And behind him was nothing but endless desert, or so he thought. He had made a torch out of burning deadwood and walked as far out as he could without losing sight of his fire. He walked for miles. There was no sign that the landscape changed or that he was going anywhere different than dry, forgotten, dark desert.

It was the cold, more than anything else that forced him back to the fire at the cave's mouth. He was wearing a red t-shirt and tan cargo shorts. His shirt had the logo of his favorite basketball team on the front, the Grandville Tigers, and the number of his favorite player on the back.

Number nine, Big Mike Morgan. On his feet he wore a pair of flip-flops and his toes were freezing.

The thought of returning to the six thirty drove him to set the timepiece several more times, but it would stubbornly reset itself to three o'clock. For some reason, the pocket watch wanted him to be *here,* and to do *something.*

But there was nowhere else to go... except into the cave.

Reuben didn't like caves. He liked treehouses. He liked to be high up in the clean air. He liked to be able to see the world around him. He liked to be high above his problems, where the birds tumbled and played and the world of adults couldn't intrude on his imagination. Treehouses were an *in-between* world. A world that belonged to children. A world of forts, and campouts, and boys-only clubs, and spaceships. It was a world where bullies didn't exist, and couldn't reach you. It was a world where only a few, select, special friends would be allowed.

Caves were pretty much the opposite of all that. The only similarity that caves shared with treehouses is that they too were an *in-between* world. But a cave was a world that connected the problems of the adult world, with the unknown, forgotten, and morbid underworld.

But the cave was Reuben's only option if he wanted to get out of this horrible shadowy place.

Reuben dropped the pocket watch into the right cargo pocket of his shorts and snatched up another torch from the endless burning fire. With a fiery stick in each hand he entered the gaping black mouth of the rock monster.

A cold wind blew across his left ear and whispered, *free us Reuben.*

A second wind blew across his right ear and also whispered. *Are you the chosen one?*

Reuben shivered at the strange sounds and voices, but told himself that it was only his imagination. Deeper and deeper into the cave, the whispering voices continued their pleading. But Reuben only got angry at them and shouted. "Shut up! I'm not the chosen one, and I'm NOT going to free you. So just *shut up!*"

The voices stopped just as he came into a small chamber. Strange writings covered the walls. It looked as if a thousand different languages were all trying to tell the same story. There were also hideous drawings of strange creatures and symbols scratched onto the stone with black ink, or charcoal.

Reuben didn't care to learn about any of the ancient writings or symbols. He only wanted to find his way out, or to wherever the timepiece wanted him to go.

He just wanted to leave. Waving the torches around the chamber made his shadows do strange dances on the cave walls. Startled at the movement of his shadows, he stopped and watched.

His own black shadows moved without him. The one on the right began to wrestle with the one on the left. They grappled and punched and kicked each other. It was a terrible fight. Finally, the shadow on the left wrapped his black hands around the right shadows throat. The right shadow seemed to drop to its knees. Its mouth was open, screaming in pain and panic. But the shadows made no sound as the victor murdered the victim.

Reuben was horrified and angry at the left shadow. He screamed at it, "You bully! You murderer!"

The shadow raised its hands and shrugged its shoulders, then pointed towards the back of the cavern. When Reuben didn't look to where the shadow was pointing, it decided to walk across the wall and *lead* Reuben to the end of the stone room. He followed the black figure with his eyes as it hopped across the wall, then disappeared behind a large boulder propped up against the stone. The boulder looked oddly like a coffin stood up on its end. When Reuben peeked behind the boulder, he saw a hole in the wall just big enough to crawl through.

At first he called out, "Oh no way. I'm NOT going in there." But after taking a closer look he noticed that there was some kind of faint orange light through the hole.

He stuck the handle of one of his torches in the dirt of the chamber floor, and took the other with him as he got down on his hands and knees and crawled through the opening.

A thick warm wind blew into the hole from ahead of him and his torch was snuffed out. But he could still see the orange light ahead and continued his crawl. His heart was pounding in his chest and a couple times he thought he couldn't breathe. But he kept his eyes on the light ahead and within a few more seconds he had reached the opening.

The opening was partially blocked by a wooden crate When Reuben stood up and peeked around the crate he saw more crates. They were stacked two, three, and sometimes four high. And there were stacks everywhere. He was standing on some kind of huge wooden dock, built into the side of a mountain, and hanging several feet above a dark salty ocean.

Above him was a dark sky peppered with weak dim stars that struggled to stay alive. Clouds the color of smoke washed over the sky, floated above the sea, and created a dark grey fog that squeezed itself between all the crates.

The orange light had been coming from one of hundreds of torches that lit the dock. They also lit the wooden walkways built into the mountainside, and the hundreds of small shacks that formed a dank, eerie town.

On the side of each of the crates surrounding Reuben, there were big letters stamped in black ink that read *"Shadow Bay Exports."* And underneath the letters on each of these crates was also stamped a small black skull and crossbones.

"Oh great" Reuben moaned, "pirates."

The Spectre

Reuben had no interest meeting bloodthirsty murdering thieving pirates. In all of his adventures and make believe in his treehouse he never bothered playing he was a pirate. He hated the very idea of pirates because they were, well, sea bullies. They took what they pleased and punished those too weak to defend themselves. And what's more, they *took pleasure* in their bad behavior. That's what all the books and movies portrayed. And Reuben had no reason to believe there was anything more he needed to know.

Reuben pulled the timepiece from his pocket and tried to set it for four o'clock. But the hands slid back to three o'clock again. He was stuck here until, well, *something* happened. This was his journey and he was at the mercy of this pocket watch.

The wooden crates made for great cover. Reuben could easily go from stack to stack unseen. His flip flops made no noise and his clothes didn't make any 'swishy' sounds when he moved. So he moved down the long dock, away from the rock wall and towards the pirate town.

The air was humid and warm. It smelled like rotten fish and seaweed, with just a touch of campfire. Off to Reuben's right rose the mountain-side. It was more of a sloped cliffside that rose straight out of the ocean. Wooden walkways zigzagged up the face of the cliff and split off here and there creating a wooden web of streets. All along the streets were the shabby little buildings made out of rotten wooden planks. Towards the bottom of the cliffside town, all the wooden walkways came together to form a large wide plaza that stretched out over the ocean and connected to the dock of crates. The plaza continued on to Reuben's left, out over the water for at least a hundred yards. Floating in the water alongside the plaza was an enormous grey pirate ship.

The ship was like every other pirate ship he had seen in the movies. It had square sails, two masts, a bowsprit, and web-like ropes that crawled up the masts to wooden bucket-like crow's nests. It had a Captain's cabin with stained glass windows and elaborate woodwork around the stern (back of the ship). Above the Captain's cabin was the poop deck with a big ship's wheel to steer it. On the sides of the ship, there were square portholes that could be opened. Reuben assumed that there were cannons behind each one. There were eight portholes on each side. A big anchor was secured to the bow (front of the ship) and rigging ran in all directions between the masts and down towards the gunwales (the rails along the sides - pronounced 'gun-als').

But this ship was also *unlike* any ship he had ever seen. Every plank of wood was grey, giving the entire ship a ghostly look. And the sails that were bunched up and tied to the spars were *black*. Atop the mainmast flew the black skull and crossbones, and atop the foremast flew a red flag with the logo of Reuben's favorite basketball team, the *Grandville Tigers.* It had the face of a tiger with its mouth open, roaring.

Weird Reuben thought. *Why would a pirate ship from a different world fly a Granville Tigers flag?*

But the strangest thing of all was the masthead. At the very front of the ship, under the bowsprit, was a statue carved out of wood and painted pitch black. Reuben had seen pictures of different mastheads before. Horses, maidens, sailors, mermaids, dragons, etc. But it was difficult to see what kind of figure these strange pirates had chosen for their boat. It was too dark to tell from where Reuben crouched behind a stack of crates.

He saw no one moving on the boat, nor did he see any signs of movement or hear any noise coming from the eerie town on his right. So he quietly tiptoed down the dock to the plaza towards the boat. As he padded closer and closer to the ship, he could see the glow of lanterns coming from the portholes, and he could hear voices inside the ship. Shouting, arguing, and sometimes laughing voices floated from the grey wooden hull. Reuben carefully approached the front of the ship and gazed at the black wooden figure.

It was the skeleton of a mermaid, and as it turns out, was not made of wood at all, but bones. The hair of the mermaid hung from its skull like strands of seaweed, and its hands were tied behind its back by old rotting rope. One of the ribs had been broken inwards, as if something had stabbed this poor creature in the heart. And in the eye sockets of the skull were embedded two deep blue crystals. Reuben guessed they were most likely sapphires.

Behind the skeleton on each side of the bow (front of the ship) were wooden name plates ~ *The Spectre*

Suddenly a voice shouted from above Reuben's head, "Don't move!"

Reuben didn't bother to see who was shouting. He simply ran away at full speed, feet pounding on the dock. He raced towards the maze of walkway in the town, hoping that he might hide in one of the hundreds of shacks along the mountainside. He could hear shouting behind him from the ship, and the thud of pirate boots, two dozen at least, thundering after him. Closer and closer. His heart was thumping in his chest so hard he could barely hear the the single horn blast from the ship. It sounded like a viking horn, with a low barbaric tone that floated over his head and on towards the town ahead. Someone in the town had heard the horn blast and began ringing a bell.

The alarm had been raised and both town and ship came alive.

Reuben turned back onto the dock where the crates were stacked, hoping he might slip back through the hole in the mountain and crawl back to the safety of the dark cave cavern. He'd rather deal with misfit shadows than a town full of murdering pirates.

His foot caught the edge of a wooden crate and he smashed his bare toes.

"Ahhhh!" he shouted in pain as he tumbled forward onto the wooden dock.

His head bumped the edge of a crate on its way down, and Reuben blacked out, unconscious.

Black Slush

"Geez. Is he *ever* going to wake up?" Tiger Master moaned. He had come come down into the cargo hold every hour for the past day and a half. He was growing impatient. This strange new prisoner was obviously from Grandville, and Tiger Master wanted answers. "Can we, like, throw some water on his face or something?"

Rat Trap was sitting next to Reuben's unconscious body as it swung in a hammock. One leg dangled over the side and his mouth was wide open.

"Yeah, we've been doin' that every hour like you ordered, Tiguh."

"Well, have you, like, slapped him a little bit? I've seen that work in the movies" Tiger Master said.

"Nah" Rat Trap answered.

"Well, like *do it then.* Let's smack him out of his coma. Like, we've got things to do and we need to pirating....where's Club Dub?!" Tiger looked around and didn't his his pudgy crew mate anywhere below deck. "Club Dub! Get down here!"

The heavy thud of boots on the deck above signaled that the big oaf had heard his captain calling and was on his way. A moment later, a short stocky boy with crazy eyes and wild teeth bounced into the room.

"Club Dub?" the pudgy kid said when he arrived.

"There you are, Club Dub. I need you to, like, slap this kid. Not too hard though. Like don't break his face or anything. Just… wake him up with those like big meaty hands of yours."

Club Dub gave a sinister smile and bore his yellow rotting teeth. "Club Dub" he replied as he walked over to the hammock. He grabbed the netting to stop the swinging and raised his muscular right palm over his head.

SLAP!

Reuben did not wake up, or even stir.

"M… m… m… maybe he's d… d… dead, Cap'n" said a tall slender boy standing behind Rat Trap in the shadows. He was leaning on a wooden staff and wearing a tall black top hat. He had dark brown skin and a worried look on his face. "M… m… maybe we should… th… th… throw him o… overboard."

"Yeah" Rat Trap agreed, "before he starts to stink the place up, ya know?"

SLAP! Club Dub kept working on his own remedy.

Tiger thought about it for a second. He removed his tiger pelt hat and wiped sweat off his brow. He turned to a short boy who was standing behind him. He had perfectly groomed hair, round spectacles, and a bowtie."What do you think Chumlick? Should we give him to Old Duppy? Toss him overboard?"

"Thank you for your interest in my opinion on the matter, my good Captain." Chumlick replied in a fake British accent. "I can hardly see how we've tried absolutely everything in our arsenal to wake this intruder. Perhaps we should..."

SLAP! Another fat palm across the face from Club Dub found it's target. But Reuben lay motionless.

Chumlick continued, "My recommendation is to employ some invigorating potion. Perhaps a libation to stir his heart rate...?"

Tiger nodded in agreement with Chumlick, while all the other boys seemed confused as to what he was *actually* suggesting. They didn't have the vocabulary or education of Charles Hansworth III, aka 'Chumlick' (the grossest thing they could come up with to call him). They envied the boy for his rich parents and luxurious lifestyle. He always tried to act and talk more 'upity' than everyone else. His perfectly ironed black pants, white buttoned-up collared shirt, and his suit vest were an odd contrast to the dusty wooden planks of the *Spectre*.

"That's like, the best idea I've heard yet, Chumlick." Tiger Master said placing his hands on his hips. Then he turned back to the boy in the top hat. "Diamond Spy, bring me some *black slush!*"

SLAP!

A minute later the tall dark boy descended the steps into the cargo hold holding a leather canteen shaped like a wine bottle. It had a big fat cork jammed into the top of it, and a black skull and crossbones branded into the leather on the side.

Tiger Master jerked the bottle out of Diamond Spy's hand, "Geez, Diamond. Took you long enough" he sneered impatiently. He pulled on the cork a few times but couldn't get it out. "Geez! Come on guys! Who did this? Who jammed the cork in so tight?!"

Nobody answered. Tiger Master kept working on removing the cork pulling and cursing and biting and groaning, until finally it came out with a loud *pop.*

"Finally. Geez. From now on, nobody corks bottles too tight. Got it?" Tiger Master yelled. His face was red from working so hard at getting the bottle open, but you could still see the enormous patch of red freckles on his cheeks.

SLAP!

"Alright, Club Dub. Enough with the slapping. Hold his head back...." Tiger put the bottle to Reuben's open drooling mouth and poured in a thick black liquid.

Much of it spilled down the side of Reuben's face and over his chin.

Tiger Master and all the other misfit boys stood back and waited silently. About thirty seconds later, Reuben's eyes popped open and he sat straight up in the hammock, coughing like crazy.

Reuben came to his senses and looked around the room. A handful of strange looking kids about his age filled the cargo hold. He knew right away that he was on the *Spectre...* and that he was in trouble. He slowly slid his hand into his right cargo pocket. A terrible feeling began to crawl over him as he realized that the timepiece was not there.

"Okay, just relax kid. Let's get right down to it. I'm Tiger Master, captain of the *Spectre* and leader of the Pirates of Skuggi. And you're...."

SLAP!

"Club Dub, you idiot. Will you stop doing that? He's awake you *moron*" Tiger snapped.

"Awww.... Club Dub" Club Dub complained before lumbering up the steps to the main deck.

"Sorry about that, kid. He's not the brightest pirate on the ship." Tiger Master offered.

"Ouch" Reuben moaned as he rubbed the left side of his face. It felt like it was on fire.

"So anyway, you're obviously from Grandville. But I don't ever remember seeing *you* at the Old Town orphanage. How did you find the passage to Skuggi? And why are you wearing a Grandville Tigers shirt?"

Reuben didn't know what to say. This *Tiger Master* kid was right about him being from Grandville, but Reuben wasn't an orphan. And he didn't live in Old Town. He had heard about the orphanage of course. An eight year old orphan girl disappeared last year from the orphanage and hadn't been seen since.

All of these thoughts came crashing together in Reuben's head and he didn't know what to say or ask. Tiger was becoming impatient.

"I don't have, like, all day here kid. You gonna answer me on your own? Or do I need to, like, call Club Dub back down here and smack some answers out of you." Tiger threatened'

Reuben rubbed his face again and decided to say *something, anything* to avoid another face thrashing from that brutish meathead named 'Club Dub.'

"I'll tell you everything you want to know and more if... you give me back my pocket watch." It was a long shot. Reuben thought the chances of these bratty pirate bullies giving anything back to anyone were pretty slim.

Tiger Master rubbed his chin as a smile curled in one corner of his mouth. One eyebrow raised up and he took a step closer to Reuben for effect, "So you want to, like, make a *deal*, huh? Okay. I'll make a deal with you. How about you tell me everything I want to know, and then you can decide if you want to walk the plank or become a slave. We have a delivery to make in Hapis to the Marsh Trolls. Oh, and I'm keeping that pretty watch of yours." Tiger Master sneered as he leaned in close to Reuben's face. "Do we have a deal?"

Reuben was horrified and dared not take that deal. He thought fast and made up a lie to see if he could alter this *deal*.

"Can I make a counter offer, Captain?" Reuben said, trying to sound confident and respectful at the same time.

"I'm all ears, kid." Tiger leaned back and listened with an impatient, disinterested look on his face.

Reuben took a deep breath, then said, "I've been sent to deliver a message to you. The orphanage drew your name for adoption and there is a family coming next week. One of the kids there told me so. He told me to wear this shirt because it was the Tiger Master *flag*, or something like that. I didn't really understand what he meant but I did it anyway hoping you'd understand."

Tiger Master was stunned. A *family?* Adoption? It couldn't be true. Who wanted a rotten freckled-face troublemaking eleven year old boy from Old Town?

Reuben continue, "and there's more. The head of the orphanage knows about the passage to Skuggi. He knows you're all here and he's going to call the police and have them come here and search for that missing girl. Your pirating days will be over. I convinced him to hold off and he agreed to not send the police... if..."

"If what?" Tiger Master leaned forward anxiously. "If *what?!*"

"If I don't return with that pocket watch" Reuben continued the lie. "It belongs to the head of the orphanage."

Tiger wondered if this kid was lying, but he knew so much about Grandville, and if he wasn't lying and didn't return with the pocket watch Tiger Master and the Pirates of Skuggi would in *real trouble*.

Before Tiger could answer Reuben, a high pitched voice cracked from above decks. It was a voice Reuben had not heard yet.

"Ship ahoy!"

Tiger looked up when he heard the call then back at Reuben, "We'll talk more later. I'll consider your counter offer. For now, I've got some work to do." As he turned to run up the grey wooden steps to the deck above he asked, "What's your name anyway, kid?"

"I'm Reuben."

"That's a stupid name. We'll need to come up with something better than *that* for you." Then he motioned towards Diamond Spy, "Hey Diamond, bring

Reuben on deck to watch us have some fun. But, like, keep an eye on him."

"No p... pr... p... problem, Cap'n" the tall dark boy said from under his top hat.

Tiger turned and bounded up the steps with the bow-tied Chumlick behind him, following closely like a dependant little brother.

"Let's g... go, Rube" Diamond said and he poked Reuben in the back with his staff. "You about to s... s... see what we p... p... pirates is all about."

Reuben got to his feet and felt the rough wooden planks with his toes. His flip flops were nowhere to be found so he walked barefoot up the steps, careful not to shuffle his feet. He didn't want any splinters.

When he climbed out of the cargo hold onto the deck, a clean ocean breeze filled his lungs and a bright sun blinded him for a moment. He hadn't seen daylight for a few days. When his eyes adjusted he looked around the ship and was horrified at what was happening.

Prisoners and Slaves

Whpsh!

The crack of a whip filled the air. Dozens of short round manlike figures waddled and tumbled about. Their heads balding and their faces were covered by beards that hung to their knees. The clothes they wore were simple canvas shirts, and pants, all ripped and tattered. Looking closer, Reuben thought that they were wearing canvas potato sacks that had holes cut out for head and arms. They ran about with fear on their faces, and a glossy hopeless stare in their eyes.

They wore chains between their ankles that rattled and scraped the deck as they scurried about the deck.

These little dwarven men were slaves.

They were pulling on ropes, scrubbing decks, moving equipment here and there. And everytime one of the pirates cracked the whip over their heads, the dwarven slaves would move just slightly faster for short time, then settle back into a slow steady compliance.

Whpsh! Club Dub cracked his mean black whip over the head of a handful of slaves at the front of the ship. They appeared to be all lined up, hauling a halyard (a rope that raises and lowers the sail). The whip snapped against the back of a slave and his shirt split wide open. Blood began to bead in a long strip across the back of his shoulder. He yelped in pain, which made Club Dub smile. But the rest of the slaves stopped pulling the rope, and turned to comfort their fallen comrade.

"Rope!" Club Dub screamed, "Pull!" But the slaves didn't pull. Reuben saw Club Dub rear back and raise the whip above his head.

Whpsh! Another slave dropped to the deck and cried out in pain. The rest were all huddled together in fear, the rope lying at their feet, and the sail above flapping wildly from the foremast.

Tiger Master yelled from the poop deck, "Club Dub! Get that sail up. If you can't get the Pogs to do it, then grab the rope and do it yourself."

Club Dub raised his arm again, preparing to whip the huddled slaves, or "Pogs" as the pirates called them, but other slaves ran from the back of the ship, grabbed the rope and began pulling. They formed a line in between the brutish crazy-eyed pirate and the bleeding huddled Pogs.

Reuben spun around and looked up at Tiger Master, "Why are you doing this? Can't you guys sail the ship yourselves?"

Tiger raised one eyebrow, "And why would I want to like, do that? Like, that's... what slaves are for... to do the grunt work so we pirates can like, do our piratey stuff."

"What piratey stuff" Reuben thought that was a dumb word, *piratey.*

Tiger motioned for Reuben to come up on the poop deck. "I'll show you."

Reuben climbed the steps and stood next to the giant wooden ship's wheel. Chumlick had his hands on the spokes of the wheel and was looking ahead, making tiny little corrections left, and right, then right, then left.

Tiger walked over to the rail of the ship and Reuben followed.

"Look kid" Tiger said, "I know this is all new and strange. So, let me explain. The Pogs are our slaves. Down in the cargo hold we have about a seventy-five more of them chained up and ready for delivery."

"Delivery?" Reuben gasped.

"Yep. We're on our way to a place called Hapis, to trade these slaves for supplies. The supplies keep us sailing and allow us to trade in other places for other supplies. We're like, *traders* more than we are pirates."

Reuben didn't buy it. And the look on his face must have shown that.

"Okay, okay. When the *occasional* ship passes by, we sometimes do some like, raiding and plundering." Tiger took a breath, raised a looking glass to his eye and continued talking as he peered out over the waves. "We keep some of the Pogs. We don't like, trade *all* of them. We're just kids, and this is like, a *huge* boat. We're not going to do all the work and maintenance..."

"Right" Reuben scoffed, "you're going to do the *'piratey'* stuff. So, where do the Pogs come from?"

"We kidnap them from Sirihbaz. That place is like, crawling with Pogs." Tiger said casually. "We sail in at night, go ashore, and just, well, take them. For as strong as they are, you'd think they'd fight back. But they're workers more than they are fighters. And a Pog will do whatever you tell them to do if you threaten them."

Whpsh! Club Dub was driving the slaves to work faster with his whip.

"Club Dub!" Tiger yelled across the ship. Club Dub turned his head and looked at his captain just before he cracked another slave across the back. "Don't damage the merchandise, you idiot!"

"Awww... Club Dub" the stout kid replied.

"You might want to watch yourself on this ship, Robin. Ole 'Clubby' can like, get carried away sometimes" Tiger giggled.

"Reuben."

"What's that?" Tiger asked

"My name is Reuben, not Robin."

Tiger rolled his eyes, "You really need a better name. That one is really dumb. I'll have the boys like, come up with one for you after we get done."

"Get done? Done with *what?*"

Tiger handed the looking glass to Reuben and pointed to a tiny black speck on the horizon.

Reuben closed one eye and looked through the glass. A tiny ship, that looked like an oversized rowboat with two triangular sails bobbed in and out of sight.

"Done with *that*" Tiger Master said. "We're going to do some of our *piratey* stuff now. I'd like for you to stay close to me please... unless you want to just stay below decks with the slaves and like hide from all the action... like a chicken."

Tiger barked more orders to his pirates, who then barked the the orders at the slaves running about the decks doing all the work.

The big black square sails were taken down, and replaced with old rotted and tatted grey sails. And Tiger ordered that the pirate flag and Tiger flag be lowered. They untied several sheets (ropes that keep the sails tight) and let them blow freely in the wind.

They made the ship look like it had been lost in a storm, damaged, abandoned, and uncared for. Tiger then looked through his glass one more time at the distant boat.

"Yep" he said gleefully, "They're coming over here." He looked up to the crow's nest, high above the tattered flapping mainsails, put his hand to his mouth, and yelled, "Get down here Pimple Tom. They're coming."

A tall skinny teenager climbed out of the crow's nest bucket, and crawled down the shrouds (the ropes that look like nets that go up to the top of the mast). When

Pimple Tom made it all the way down to the deck, he bounded up the steps to the poop deck.

"Here Cap'n" he said with a lazy salute. Pimple Tom was a pale, red headed teenager. His face was covered with red pimples and sores. The pimples ran down his neck, all over his shoulders, and he even had pimples on his small chest. He was a head taller than the other boys, but he slouched so badly when stood that you couldn't tell. He wore no shirt, only a pair of canvas shorts with a red sash tied around his waist. And he was so skinny Reuben could just barely see his ribs. His neck and the tops of his shoulders were pink from sunburn.

"Tommy, my boy, this is the new kid.... Robin, or Robert."

"It's *Reuben.*"

"Whatever" Tiger smiled. Reuben thought he was just doing it on purpose now. "And this is Pimple Tom, my first mate."

"Howdy." Pimple Tom said in the deepest Southern accent Reuben had ever heard.

Pirates don't say 'howdy.' Reuben thought, *these are kids are the worst pirates ever.*

When they were done with the introductions, Tiger called up Rat Trap who emerged from the cargo hold with all kinds of weapons and gadgets. Each boy was handed a crossbow and a bunch of iron bolts. But they all had something unique as well. Tiger Master carried what he called *'the axe of fury.'* It was a staff four feet long, with a silver axe head. The silver was engraved with all kinds of strange, almost magical etchings and scroll works. Pimple Tom had a long curved sword, a cutlass. It was rusted in places and had dings and chips in its blade. Diamond Spy carried a long staff with a blue crystal tied to the end with twine. It looked a child's pretend wizard staff. Chumlick, the prim and proper pirate, carried a small rapier (a thin-bladed fencing sword with a bell shaped handguard). He said that it was a 'gentleman's weapon.' Club Dub the wonder-thug, carried not one, but two baseball bats, each with a dozen iron studs embedded in the ends. Rat Trap carried a wicked looking knife, and also had a small wooden cube the size of a coffee mug dangling from his belt.

"Pimple Tom, secure all the Pogs below deck, the rest of you, hide yourselves and load your crossbows."

"Aye Captin." they all said in unison.

"Oh, and Tommy boy? Fetch me a Pog to use as bait."

Reuben didn't like it all when Tiger Master said *fetch me a Pog*. But it wouldn't be the last time he heard the phrase.

Ghost Ship

Reuben had no weapon. But he was crouched down with the pirates, hiding behind the gunwale (the railing along the sides of a ship). Tiger Master had ordered that the *Spectre* drift freely and unmanned in the middle of the ocean.

With all of the slaves below in the cargo hold, and all of the pirates hiding from view, the big wooden grey vessel almost look like a ghost ship.

The *Trollhammer* came within about fifty yards of the *Spectre* when Pimple Tom crawled up the steps of the poop deck and peeked over the gunwale for a look. He made a few silent hand signals to Tiger Master, who turned and whispered to the line of hiding pirate boys.

"Thirty-four men. Probably Diambi's navy. Looks like they have a prisoner." Tiger Master looked back to Tom who made a few more signals then snuck back down to join the rest of the boys on the main deck.

"Load crossbows" Tiger whispered to everyone, who quickly loaded the bolts into the iron cradles of their weapons, then cranked the strings back, locking them into place.

Reuben was a kind of impressed at how quickly and orderly the boys did this. For as terrible they seemed at talking and acting like pirates, they performed their duties in a very disciplined and orderly way.

Pimple Tom took Tiger's spot, and Tiger Master crawled up the steps to the poop deck and waited there alone, hidden from view.

Tom peeked one more time over the rail, then nodded to up Tiger.

"Deploy the Pog" he whispered.

Rat Trap put a little wooden step stool next to the railing. He then tugged a rope that was secured around a slave's neck. The Pog had been sitting on the cargo holds steps, his stout little hands bound behind his back and his mouth gagged with a dirty white cloth. His long dirty white beard hung over his knees. The Pog stood up and waddled over to the step.

Reuben heard a man's voice call out. It was deep and confident. It was the commanding voice of an adult. "Ahoy there!.. Captain Thorne of Diambi's Hapis Navy. We've come to assist... anyone there?"

There were more voices coming from the *Trollhammer*, murmurs of conversation that Reuben and the pirates could hear from their hidden position.

Captain Thorne's voice was deep and booming, even when he tried to speak quietly. Tiger Master overheard him saying, "secure the *Trollhammer* to the side of the ship. We're going to board her."

Two loud *clanks* were heard as grappling hooks from the *Trollhammer* landed on the decks of the *Spectre*, one near the foremast, and other close to the poop deck's steps. Their iron teeth bit into the greying wood as their ropes were tightened by the unsuspecting men below.

Tiger nodded and Rat Trap pulled out his terrible knife and poked the Pog in the back. The dwarven man obediently stood up on the step and into the view of the *Trollhammer*, who had now drifted alongside the *Spectre* and was preparing to board. Then Pimple Tom tossed a rope ladder over the side, which tumble as it unrolled along the side the *Spectre's* hull.

After of few moments of restive silence, Reuben heard Thornes rough voice.

"Ahoy there!" Thorne called up, "We'd like permission to come aboard, dwarf."

The Pog said nothing. He stood terrified, bound and gagged, with Rat Traps knife pressing on his fat little back.

"I said we'd like to board, with your permission... Answer me, dwarf! Do you need assistance? Can we board?"

Tiger Master slipped his tiger pelt hat on his head and shouted "Permission granted Captain."

All at once the pirates leapt to their feet and pointed their crossbows over the side of the ship and down at the sailors.

After a *very* uncomfortable few seconds of stunned silence Thorne demanded to know who was in charge?

Tiger Master jumped up and boldly yelled, "I am!... Tiger Master, at your service" he gave a mocking bow, "and you, Captain Thorne, are my prisoner."

Thorne growled something about dying before being taken prisoner and Reuben thought *how stupid can you be, Thorne? Dying doesn't save anybody.*

Tiger Master then ordered Pimple Tom to 'raise the colors' and the skinny redhead furiously pulled a line that lifted the black flag of piracy into the air.

"You are now the prisoners of the Pirates of Skuggi" Tiger proclaimed, "You will be taken aboard our ship, where your fates will be determined by my crew according to the laws of piracy and the pleasure of Old Duppy. If you do not surrender peacefully, we will kill everyone one of you and burn your ship to ash.... You have only a moment to decide Captain Thorne... Do you surrender?"

"Of course not, you bratty little toad!" Thorne screamed.

Tiger nodded to Chumlick, who yanked the iron trigger of his crossbow. The bolt zipped out at lightning speed and lodged itself into the chest of one of Thorne's sailors. The man tumbled backwards over the side of the *Trollhammer*, being hit so hard by the bolt that he was dead before he even hit the water.

"I don't think you understand the situation, Cap'n Thorne" Tiger said calmly with a wicked grin on his freckled face, "We'll pick you off one at a time until you surrender. You'll be the last one to die, that way you can watch all of your men suffer first."

Reuben was stunned. He had never seen a man die before. He balled up his fists to shake out the trembles in his hands and arms.

"Alright! Alright... I surrender" Thorne conceded. A visible wave of relief washed over the crew of the *Trollhammer*, except for the hooded prisoner at the front of the ship.

"You and your crew will come aboard and be clapped in irons," Tiger Master ordered. "Your prisoner also belongs to me, now. After you've had a chance to like, settle down, you and I can discuss terms."

One by one the crew of the *Trollhammer* climbed the rope ladder, until half of them were aboard. Tiger Master then ordered Thorne to come aboard with his prisoner, and leave the remaining half of his crew on the *Trollhammer*. Pimple Tom and Rat Trap then pulled the rope ladder back up to make sure the sailor couldn't board when no one was looking.

Reuben watched from the front of the ship, and wished that he was somewhere else, *anywhere* else at that moment. He knew things were about to get a lot worse and wondered if jumping on to the *Trollhammer* would be safer than staying aboard the *Spectre*. He looked at the helpless fifteen sailors in the longboat, separated from their captain and crewmates with no ability to row away to safety.

Then something in the water caught his eye. It was a red light. It wasn't red water or a hazy patch of kelp. It was more like a bright red lightbulb the size of a basketball... and it was moving in circles around and beneath the *Trollhammer*. Another light appeared, then another. They circled and darted in slow graceful spurts. Reuben knew instantly that the lights were coming from strange sea creatures, but they were too deep under the surface for him to see the shape of their bodies. He could only see the lights.

Even in broad daylight, he could see them moving about. The men of on the *Trollhammer* saw them too, and began shrieking in fear. They called up to their captain for help, but Thorne was occupied. He had his own problems to deal with right then.

Thorne and his group of unarmed sailors huddled together in the center of the main deck between the *Spectre's* foremast and mainmast. Tiger Master descended the poop deck steps, like an arrogant king descending from his throne, and stood before Thorne. He held his loaded crossbow with one hand, and in his other hand was the 'axe of fury.'

"Please act like a grown up and like, behave yourself, Captain" he said with a mocking respect.

Thorne looked all around him and realized that he and fifteen grown men (and his hooded prisoner) were being held captive by *only six armed boys.*

It was too much for his pride to handle and he lurched for Tiger Master, one arm raised to cover his face, and the other stretched out to grab the boy pointing a crossbow at him.

"Attack!" Tiger Master shouted as he skipped backwards and tumbled up the poop deck steps and fired his crossbow.

All six crossbows fired at once, and five grown men dropped to the deck, dead... but Thorne wasn't hit.

Fight on the Spectre

When Thorne leapt for Tiger Master, the ship exploded with action. Thorne's men spread out all over the deck trying to grab the pirate boys, many of them pairing up as it was two grown unarmed men to one armed pirate boy.

Reuben noticed right away that Thorne's prisoner was knocked over by one of the falling men who had been struck by a crossbow bolt. When the prisoner hit the ground he flipped over onto his hands and knees and scurried to the side of the boat, and alongside the railing. He eventually crawled to the wooden poop deck steps and hid underneath them while the violence played out.

Club Dub was swinging his baseball bats like a crazed gorilla. The two men in front of him walked backwards dodging the wild boys assaults but not gathering the nerve to jump in close and grab him. Club Dub was grinning ear-to-ear and laughing like the kid was let loose in a toy store with a one hundred dollar bill. His teeth bright yellow, and his eyes slightly offset, gave him the look of a maniac who had escaped the loony bin and was on his next murderous rampage.

Pimple Tom had a harder fight. The men in front of him crowded him into a corner at the front of the ship, near

Reuben. When Pimple Tom thrust his cutlass at one man, the other would reach in and try to grab him. Being in a corner, there wasn't enough room to get a good wide swing of the blade, a cutlass' most effective use. And Pimple Tom was skinny. The weight of his weapon quickly became too much for him to handle, and Reuben saw him tire quickly. Finally one of the men grabbed Pimple Tom by the wrist, while the other threw a punch into the boy's face so hard, they thought he was dead.

The man who had grabbed Pimple Tom's wrist was no longer unarmed. He snatched up the cutlass, spun around and attacked the first pirate boy he saw... unfortunately for him, it was Diamond Spy.

The tall dark-skinned boy moved around the ship, dodging the adults with ease. He was 'light-of-foot,' as they say, gracefully danced around the cutlass' blade when the man made his first thrust. Diamond's staff twirled, as he spun in a full circle. The blue gem tied to the end of the staff landed on the swordsman's cheek with a loud thud, and Reuben saw a brief flash of blue light from the gem on contact. The man himself stepped back, half stunned that the boy actually hit him, and half impressed at his skills. He put his hand to his cheek where the gem had hit him and drew it away. His hand was covered with warm salt water instead of blood. More water began to gush from the man's face. He dropped the sword and put both hands to his cheek to stop the fountain of salt water spewing from the side of his face. He began to shriek so loudly that other men and boys nearby, stopped their fighting for a few horrible seconds and looked. The man's head dissolved into a bubble of water that burst open and spilled down the man's chest. Then his chest collapsed and spilled down over his legs, then his legs liquified as well. Only the sword, some sailor's clothes, and a puddle of stinky water remained where a grown man once stood. Diamond bowed as he removed his tophat and placed it over his heart in a sign of respect for his fallen enemy. Or maybe he was bowing to the audience men and boys that saw him perform his magic.

When two sailor's nearby saw the terrible magic of Diamond Spy, they abandoned the fight and jumped over the side of the ship. One of them was pulled aboard the *Trollhammer* by their terrified comrades, the other was pulled into the deep dark ocean by the red lights. He did not resurface.

As Diamond finished his long bow, a sailor snuck up behind him.

"Diamond! Watch out... behind you!" Reuben shouted. *Why did I just do that? Why did I try to help a pirate?* Reuben immediately thought.

Diamond turned and backed away as the man grabbed the fallen cutlass and swung it at his head. Diamond parried the swing with his staff, the wood blocking the blade from reaching his neck. But the blade bit deep into the staff, and when the man pulled away, Diamond's staff was yanked right out of his hand. He stepped back away from the armed sailor, who was seething with both fear and anger. Having no other weapon, Diamond held his top hat with both hands. The head hole of the hat pointed at the sailor, and the top of the hat in front of Diamond's chest. The man immediately went for the kill and thrust the point of the sword at the boy. The the sword went through the hat, and Reuben saw the sailor push it so far through that only the handle could be seen. But oddly, the sword did not exit Diamond's back, nor did Diamond look like he was in pain at all.

The confused sailor pulled his sword back, retracting it out of the hat. And when the sword fully exited the tophat, there was *a sandwich stuck on the end near the tip of the blade.*

The sailor stood wide-eyed, paralyzed with confusion. Diamond Spy smiled and said, "M.... m... my lu... l... lunch. Th... thanks." And grabbed the ham sandwich, sliding it off the blade, then taking a big bite. He then reached his hand into his tophat and pulled out his staff. Reuben blinked. He had just seen his staff on the other side of the ship lying on the deck. *How in the world did he....*

Crack! The confused sailor was hit on the side of his face with the gem at the end of Diamond's magic staff and he tumbled over the gunwale. But he liquified before he even hit the ocean water below. He didn't fall into the sea, he *rained* on it.

The spectacular magic of Diamond Spy frightened many of the remaining sailors to give up the fight and jump back into the *Trollhammer.*

Thorne's Demise

Captain Thorne didn't take notice of the magic, nor did he care. He had killed hundreds of Marsh Trolls in the past, and even a few men. He was no stranger to magic, killing, or the chaotic haze of battle. He wrestled with Tiger Master on the poop deck. Tiger was on his back, and Thorne was towering over him. Both of them had their hands on Tiger's 'axe of fury.' Thorne was yanking violently at the axe and Tiger was being shaken so hard by the pulling that his tiger pelt hat come off.

"Heeeeelp!" Tiger yelled, his voice dripping with fear and panic.

Rat Trap appeared, seemingly, out of nowhere and Reuben saw the tip of his knife vanish into the back of Thorne's right thigh.

Thorne hollered more in surprise than pain and released one hand from the axe handle and struck Rat Trap in the nose with the back of his fist. The boy tumbled backwards, blood gushing from his nostrils, hands covering his nose and mouth. His eyes watered shut and he fell to his knees. Then Thorne grabbed Tiger by his hair. Tiger let go of the axe so he could use his hands to get away, and it was just what Thorne was hoping he'd do. Thorne wrenched the axe free and held it above his head with his right hand, Tiger hair was clutched firmly in his left hand.

Diamond Spy and Chumlick were at the front of the boat, and could not get to the poop deck fast enough. Rat Trap was blinded by a broken nose. Pimple Tom lay unconscious on the main deck, and Club Dub was busy swinging his bats at sailors in a rage.

Reuben saw movement on the poop deck steps just then; a flurry of grey movement and a flash of red hair, as the hooded prisoner ran across the poop deck and tackled Thorne just before the axe came down on Tiger's head.

The surprised Thorne held his hands and arms up over his head, but the redheaded stranger thrashed at him. His lips pulled back in a vicious sneer as he pummeled fist after fist into Captain Thorne's face and neck. Eventually, Thorne's only movement was from the impact of the blows. He was knocked out, cold. As the prisoner continued to beat at Thorne's unconscious body, the remaining sailors jumped back into the

Trollhammer. They cut the ropes attaching it to the *Spectre* and opened up the big triangular sails.

The pirate boys gathered together on the poop deck and watched the prisoner thrash and thrash until he was completely tired out. He dismounted Thorne's body and rolled over onto the deck, His eyes shut and he laughed wildly at the sky above.

I think we may have found someone crazier than Club Dub, Reuben thought.

As the *Trollhammer* began to distance itself from the *Spectre*, Thornes unconscious body was tossed overboard. The sailors grabbed it and pulled him into the longboat. Red lights swarmed underneath the *Trollhammer* as it began to sail away. Those creatures seemed to know where their next meal would come from.

Tiger Master was beside himself with bitter anger at Thorne and the sailors. But especially Thorne. He hated that man for the violent way he tried to take over the *Spectre*.

"That dog!" Tiger screamed. "I gave him a chance to live. I was going to offer terms. But he just... like... *had* to fight. *Had* to fight back and turn this whole ordeal into like, one huge turd bouquet."

The Pirates of Skuggi all laughed together, but Tiger was being serious.

"Rat Trap..."

"I'm here, Captain. Whatcha need?"

Tiger stared at the escaping *Trollhammer* and sneered at them. With cold deep hatred he said, "Deploy the cube."

"Da cube? You sure about dat, Cap?" Rat Trap asked hesitantly.

"I'm sure Ratty, my boy." Tiger said almost gleefully.

Rat Trap ran down the steps into the cargo hold and started rooting around for something. Reuben could hear boxes and various things falling to the floor, and bottles breaking below deck.

"Rat Trap, you junk-monger!" Tiger yelled, "Hurry up, they're getting away!"

A moment later Rat Trap bounced up the steps again carrying an oversized crossbow-like contraption. The cradle where a bolt would go was about three inches wide... just big enough for the wooden cube that Rat Trap untied from his belt. He placed the small cube in the cradle, then took a small brass key and inserted it in a tiny keyhole. As he twisted the key around and around, Reuben heard tiny gears and springs in the cube start to work. There was a clicking sound coming from the cube, and it reminded Reuben of the tick-tick of his stolen timepiece.

With the cube activated, Rat Trap jammed a large crank into the crossbow and wound it until the thick cord was pulled all the way back to the trigger. He and Tiger lifted the crossbow and rested the front of it on the rail. Rat Trap gazed through a brass sight ring and calculated the distance to the *Trollhammer*. He licked his forefinger and held it up to gauge the speed and direction of the wind.

"All set, Captain... by da way, how many men are on dat boat" he said in his snarky Brooklyn accent.

"B... b...b bout f... fifteen, I'd say" Diamond said.

"Diamond's probably right" Tiger Master said, "Fifteen men."

Rat Trap pulled the trigger and the crossbow launched the cube into the air with a loud low *thwunk*.

As the cube arched through the sky, Club Dub, of all people, sang out a melody in a loud high-pitched voice, "Fifteen men on a dead man's chest..."

That's from Treasure Island! Reuben knew the classics well enough to recognize the popular pirate song.

"...yo, ho, ho and a bottle of rum" all the boys replied in unison.

The cube landed in the middle of the *Trollhammer*. A sailor picked it up and looked at it. They must have thought it was supposed to explode but didn't work properly. The men on the *Trollhammer* were heard laughing. But their laughter turned into cries of terror. The cube popped open and began spinning like a top. The sailor dropped it in surprise and watched as tiny saw blades slid out the side and bit into the wooden bottom of the hull. The cube drilled straight down and bore a hole right through the hull. A fountain of water sprayed straight up and flooded the longboat.

Red lights swarmed the water around the *Trollhammer* as it disappeared under the waves, and the sailors' last cries vanished in watery gurgles.

Dracula

Tiger ordered that the Pogs be brought on deck. The ship was repaired from the dings, scrapes and cuts that the battle had worn into her. Rat Trap was in charge of the *Spectre's* maintenance. The tattered sails were brought down and the big black square sails were raised.

"Set out course for Hapis, Chumlick."

"Aye-aye, Captain" the prim and proper pirate said as he spun the helm to starboard.

Tiger Master retired to his Captain's cabin, while Reuben leaned on the rail of the poop deck and watched the water rush by. He felt uneasy at the sight of red lights in their wake. *Those creatures are following us!*

The breeze was cool and stiff, and the sun was direct, but not too hot. Reuben closed his eyes and enjoyed the slow tossing of the ship over the sea swells as they rolled past.

When he opened his eyes and looked down at the surface of the water, he saw a reflection... it wasn't *his* reflection though. He had lost his reflection in the two o'clock world. The reflection staring back at him was from the redheaded stranger that had gone mad fighting Thorne.

"So, how long have you been on this crazy ship?" the stranger asked.

Reuben watched him carefully. He was leaning on the rail to Reuben's right, arms crossed, with his chin on his wrists.

"Only a few days" said Reuben.

"New guy, huh? Well, that explains why you didn't help out much during the fight."

"I'm not much of a fighter." Reuben was a little irritated at the insult.

"Take it easy, kid. I know you're not a member of these *Pirates of Skuggi.* What I don't know is why you're on this ship." The redheaded teen turned and looked Reuben directly in the eye with one arrogant eyebrow raised.

Reuben didn't answer. There was no way he was about to trust some crazy violent teenager with the truth of why he was stuck here.

The redhead leaned in close, right up to Reuben's ear and said in a low menacing voice, "Have you happened to see my pocket watch laying around here anywhere?"

Reuben jumped when he said *pocket watch*. Trembling he asked the stranger, "How did you... I mean... what makes you think I know anything about a pocket watch?"

"You have no reflection. It's as plain as the nose on that scared little face of yours, kid. You lost your reflection in the shadow dimension. My guess is, you've lost the timepiece and you're *stuck* here."

Reuben's heart was pounding a million miles an hour. His jaw was clenched shut and he was too scared to think of what to say.

"Don't worry, kid. I'll help you find the missing timepiece. Maybe we can *both* get out of here."

Fat chance, you psycho. But Reuben just forced a fake laugh, "Yeah, sure. Great."

The boy looked off into the horizon, "What's your name anyway, kid?"

"Reuben."

"Reuben?! That's a dumb name. You need something more exciting since you're stuck on a pirate ship..." They looked down at the surface of the water again, but only one reflection looked back up at them. "I got it! *Dracula!* That the perfect name for you. You have no reflection, just like the old vampire himself."

Before Reuben could protest, the redheaded teen stuck his hand out for a shake and said, "My name is Petros O' Magos. I have many titles, but back in the six-thirty my real name is Pete Smith.... Friends call me 'Smitty.'"

Reuben faked a smile and shook Smitty's hand.

"Don't worry, Dracula. We're gonna find *our* timepiece and get off this wooden hunk of junk."

Right then, Pimple Tom lumbered up the steps to the poop deck and motioned for Smitty and Reuben.

"Cap'n wants to see ya'll. I'll take you to his cabin." Tom turned and plodded back down the steps. The two boys followed him to the single door the led from the main deck, into Tiger Master's cabin. When the door was shut behind them, Tiger Master told them to sit down. They sat a long wooden table with eight chairs. Three were on each side, and one was at each end. Tiger sat on the end, at the head of the table, of course. Reuben sat in on the side in the middle chair, and Smitty walked to the other end of the table and sat at the head of that end.

Tiger Master glared at Smitty. He was a little insulted that a teenager would just waltz into *his* cabin, on *his* ship and sit at the head of *his* table.

"I wanted you to know that like, the crew has all voted to make you both... members" Tiger Master said. "Of course we can't force you to be. But you have the choice of either joining our crew, or... we can trade you as a slave to the Marsh Trolls once we get to Hapis."

Smitty straighten up in his chair nervously. "I'm not going back to Hapis. The last thing I need is to get caught up with the Frumps. I think they've had enough of me."

"What's like, the story there? Did you get in trouble with the Marsh Trolls? Is King Boglack looking for you?" Tiger Master asked suspiciously.

"Something like that. I'd rather go back to Skuggi with you guys. So, if it's alright, I'll take you up on your offer to join the crew."

"Great" Tiger said, "by the way like, what's your name anyway."

"Smitty."

"That's a dumb name. We'll have to come up with something better than that for you." Tiger snorted then turned to Reuben. "And what about you, Rupert? You gonna like, join my crew?"

"Reuben."

"Right. Robert" Tiger grinned.

"Reuben. Rooo... bin."

"Don't get sassy with me, Rooster" Tiger snickered.

Reuben rolled his eyes, and was going to give Tiger an answer, but Smitty cut in and said, "Captain Tiger Master, I think I have the perfect new name for Reuben over here... what do ya'll think of *Dracula?*"

Tiger Master didn't even think about it for a second before he shouted, "Yes! *Anything* is better than 'Reuben'" He used quotation fingers when he *finally* said Reuben's name correctly.

"What d'ya say, Dracula? Will you join my crew?"

It was the only option Reuben had if he ever wanted to find the pocket watch and get away from these moronic pirates... and Smitty.

"Count me in... *Captain.*"

Wormpools

Smitty stayed on board the *Spectre* while Chumlick, Tiger, and Pimple Tom escorted the seventy-five WolliPog slaves onto the dock. The Marsh Troll town was buzzing with excitement, and its inhabitants were grunting, snarling and yelling at each other. Half of the slaves were auctioned off for gold. The other half were traded in-bulk with King Boglack. In exchange, He gave the Pirates of Skuggi twenty crates of black slush.

The only thing the Pirates of Skuggi loved more than black slush, was gold, and action.

When they set sail again They scanned the horizon for more ships. But the seas around Hapis were quiet that day and there would be no pirating anytime soon.

Smitty and Reuben sat in the front of the ship, leaning over the sides. They were deep in a conversation about the red lights that had been following the *Spectre*. Reuben didn't like them at all, especially at night when they swarmed around the boat, casting a red glow up the side of the ship's hull as they circled and waited.

Pimple Tom was up in the crow's nest keeping watch, while Chumlick was at the helm. Club Dub was asleep, curled up in a pile of ropes and nets at the foot of the foremast, while Rat Trap was sitting on the steps of the poop deck, sharpening his knife.

All was quiet until Tiger Master burst out of his cabin.

"Gather around, everyone. We need to talk." he yelled. The crew began to gather around Tiger Master on the main deck. Club Dub was woken up by Smitty, who kicked him in the butt as he walked by.

"There's been a change in our plans and I wanted to like, see what you guys think" Tiger began. He looked at Reuben and Smitty and said, "so you newbies are filled in, we normally take our treasure and sail to the Wild Isles. We like, camp out for a few days, drink lots of black slush, hunt, fish, and relax for a few days. Before we leave, we bury our treasure. We got a good haul from Hapis, and King Boglack, the Marsh Troll king was extra generous with the payment of our black slush. Well, he and I spent some time like, talking about a big score I think we should try..." Everyone was quiet as Tiger took a deep breath, then said, "I want to find Neptune's treasure."

"But I thought Neptune's treasure was a myth, Tiguh" Rat Trap said.

"I don't think it is at all. I think it's like, *real.*"

"Boglack said that it's hidden on the Island of Isango" Tiger said hesitantly.

The boys gasped all at once.

"My dear Captain, I was under the impression, as were all of my shipmates I'm sure, that the Island of Isango has been dealt some terrible curse. From what we have deduced from our various travels, the island is quite unreachable by ship." Chumlick was standing straight and tall, pointing his finger into the air as he talked in his fake British accent. "It is quite impossible."

"*Nothing* is impossible" Tiger said. "There's got to be some kind of like, shortcut, or magic, or something. And I want to find it. *Think about it*, guys. Like, we could discover a whole new world. And we've only tried to sail there once. It's not like we've really done everything we can."

"Well, guess you're right, Cap. I'm in. I'd like to try somethin' new for a change" said Pimple Tom as he rubbed his bruised face.

"Sure. Why not. Let's do it," said Rat Trap.

Chumlick nervously folded his arms and looked down at his feet, "I concede."

"What about you Clubby?" Tiger asked.

"Club Dub" the stout boy said yawning.

Smitty and Reuben nodded in agreement as well.

Tiger called for Diamond Spy who had taken the helm while everyone talked. "They're all on board, Diamond. It's time."

Diamond nodded and left the ship's wheel, and walked to the front of the ship. Tiger himself took over steering.

When he got to the helm, he yelled "Rat Trap... *fetch me a Pog.*"

Rat Trap hurried below deck into the cargo hold and returned with a dwarven slave. It was an old WolliPog with with a thick brown beard that was turning silver at its roots. The dwarf's hands were tied behind his back, and had a lead rope around his neck.

Diamond Spy turned his back to the crew and stood at the very tip of the bow. He raised his arms out over the water, his staff in his right hand. He began chanting loudly in some strange language. Reuben noticed that while he chanted that he didn't stutter. His chanting grew louder as the blue gem on the end of his wizard's staff began to glow intensely. The deep blue gems in the eye sockets of the skeleton mermaid, tied to the front of the ship, also began to glow.

Diamond's chanting grew louder. Reuben heard splashing sounds coming from the water and peeked over the railing. Hundreds of red lights were darting around at the surface of the water, churning the water. He could see the bodies of the creatures slithering in slimy masses around each other. They had tentacles like giant squid, and their heads reminded him of the heads of hammerhead sharks, only slightly deformed. Protruding from their heads were long antennas, from which dangled glowing red sacks the size of a basketball.

The creatures were slapping the water with their tentacles and snapping their jaws in a frenzy, waiting to be fed. They swarmed in an enormous glowing red school on one side of the ship.

"Smitty" Tiger ordered, "Toss that Pog to Old Duppy."

The other boys watched excitedly as Smitty grabbed the WolliPog slave by his shirt and escorted him to the side of the ship. Rat Trap extended a long wooden plank out over the churning bubbling water below. The creatures were practically jumping out of the water. Smitty pushed the Pog onto the plank, but the poor little dwarf fell to his knees in fright.

"We've got a *kneeler*," Pimple Tom laughed.

This is awful! Reuben thought. *I can't stand to watch. This is wrong. This is so wrong.*

Tiger yelled again, "Smitty, toss the Pog to Old Duppy. If I have to like, come down there and do it myself, you're going with him!"

The pirates drew out their weapons and stood behind Smitty. He had no choice. Smitty the crazy redheaded stranger, didn't look so terrifying all of a sudden. He looked *terrified*.

Diamond's chanting was getting louder and the blue gem was blazing so hot and bright that it was almost white! The creatures were beside themselves with hunger and excitement.

Smitty nervously walked out on the plank, picked the Pog up by the back of his collar and drug him back onto the deck.

"Do it you yourselves" he said as he stared down the armed boys.

Tiger jumped down onto the main deck, cursing and whining as he pushed himself past the pirates. He shoved Smitty aside and grabbed the slave by the arm. He pulled the dwarf out onto the plank and without hesitating a second kicked him into the water.

The Pog disappeared into the mass of tentacles and teeth and seconds later the churning stopped. There was a silent calm that came over the water. You could hear a pin drop. Then a rushing roaring sound came from the front of the ship.

Tiger ran back up the poop deck steps and grabbed the ship's wheel. "Everybody, *hold on!*" he shouted.

Reuben and Smitty looked ahead of the ship and gasped as they watched an enormous whirlpool form in the waves ahead. It was as wide as a football field and rushed like a violent river. A low turbulent black cloud floated above it, and lightning struck the swirling funnel in loud cracks.

Smitty grabbed Reuben and pulled him over to the foremast where they both wrapped their arms around it, squeezing their eyes shut, and holding on for dear life.

Diamond Spy stopped chanting and held on to the railing.

The *Spectre* dove straight into the whirlpool, its bow angled down more and more with every second. It was sailing straight down. Reuben opened his eyes one last time and only saw a wall of water rushing around the ship. They were hurtling straight down.

Then everything went black. There was a strange sensation of gravity shifting in Reuben's head. And instead of falling straight down, it felt as if the ship was shooting straight *up*!

A moment later the *Spectre's* nose angled down with a huge *splash! And the ship was floating* calmly on the surface of the ocean again.

Smitty and Reuben slowly opened their eyes and looked around. The sky was bright and the ocean breeze was at their backs filling the big black sails above them. Over the port bow (front left side of the ship) two crescent moons hung side-by-side over the horizon, and directly off the starboard bow (the front right side of the boat) was a long stretch of black sky. A thick dark cloud hovered over a black island that stretched for dozens of miles in both directions under that sky.

"Welcome to the Ocean of Isango" Tiger laughed. Tiger put his hand to his mouth trying to sound like an airline pilot, "We'd like to thank you for flying *Spectre* Airways. Off to your right you'll see the island of Skuggi, our final destination. You'll noticed the captain has turned *off* the fasten seat belt sign. At this time you are free to roam about the cabin.... Flight attendants prepare for landing."

Tiger whirled the ship's wheel to the right, and the *Spectre* slowly turned its nose to the black cloud covering the island of Skuggi.

The pirates brought a dozen or so more Pogs up to the main deck and began whipping them into work, preparing the ship to dock in Shadow Bay.

Reuben looked at Smitty, leaned in close and said, "Let's find that pocket watch of ours and get the heck out of here."

Smitty nodded and said, "I'm with you, Dracula."

The Shack

Shadow Bay came alive when the *Spectre* returned. The town was a mix of humans, Marsh Trolls, and Pogs. The blobby-nosed Marsh Trolls were in charge of overseeing the slave work of expanding the village. New shacks and more lengths of wooden walkways were added higher and higher up the mountain side everyday.

The Pogs were driven down to the dock by whip, where they unloaded the crates of black slush onto the plaza, and stamped them with the skull and crossbones.

When the ship was emptied, Tiger told the boys to take a few days of rest. They would be sailing to Isango soon. The pirates went ashore, gathered at the door of a dirty little wooden shack built into the side of the mountain. Tiger Master ordered that they all remove their weapons and change their clothes, which they did, before entering the shack.

Reuben wondered what could be so special about a filthy little room. When he peeked his head in the doorway, there was no light, no furniture, and no windows. It was an empty single room with a dirt floor.

"Alright Dracula" Tiger Master said with his hands on his hips. "It's time to see if you're telling the truth."

Reuben had forgotten about the lie he told Tiger when he first came on board the *Spectre*.

Tiger Master nodded toward Diamond Spy and asked, "Diamond, will you please give Dracula his pocket watch?"

Diamond Spy nodded back, removed his top hat, and plunged his arm into it. He reached in all the way up to his shoulder. His entire arm looked like it had been lopped off and replaced by a black top hat. After a couple seconds of digging, Diamond slid his arm back out of the hat holding the timepiece.

Smitty nervously watched, and quietly stepped closer and closer to Diamond Spy without anyone noticing, while Tiger spoke.

"You said that if you didn't return with the watch, the head of the Orphanage would send the police here." Tiger grimaced at Reuben, "I won't let that happen. So, take your stupid watch back, and go home." Tiger tossed the timepiece to Reuben, and pointed into the little shack's dark room.

"Tiger, I need to tell you something" Reuben said as he wound up the timepiece and set it for four o'clock.

"What's that Dracula?" Tiger snapped.

Reuben rubbed the timepiece while he said, "I lied to you about everything! You're not being adopted. There is no family. And I never talked to the head of any orphanage. *I'm not an orphan...*" Reuben said as the sparkling particles of dust swirled around him, "I'm *not* a pirate. And my name is *REUBEN.*"

Whoosh!

Smitty tried to push himself past the boys and reach for Reuben. But he was too late. Reuben disappeared before Smitty could grab his arm, leaving him stranded with the pirates.

I can't believe the little punk left me here! I thought we were going to escape together with the timepiece. Smitty felt betrayed, crushed by Reuben's lies. Tiger

Master, for his own reasons, felt the same way.

Tiger sniffed and said, "Forget that little punk! He was a useless pirate anyway."

"I k... ki... k... kinda l...liked em, Cap'n" Diamond Spy said.

"Oh really, Duh... Duh... Diamond? Then why don't you juh... juh... join him?" Tiger mocked.

Smitty asked, "What's in the shack?"

Rat Trap answered, "The Old Town Orphanage. If you walk through dat door, you'll be taken back to our world. You'll come out the other end in a small wooden outhouse. The outhouse is hidden in the woods behind the orphanage.

Smitty grinned from ear to ear. *So this is where Skuggi's hidden portal is. But why doesn't it go directly into the Chamber of Crossroads? Perhaps there is more than one portal here!*

"Well Cap'n? We goin' home fer a while?" Pimple Tom asked. The boys all looked to Tiger Master, who was brooding and pouting about being lied to. Reuben had told him that there was a *family that wanted to adopt him.* And while he suspected that Reuben might be lying, he had carried a small flicker of hope in his heart for the past few days.

Reuben had snuffed out that hope and left them all behind.

"NO!" Tiger snapped. "Get back to the *Spectre*. We're going to find Neptune's treasure."

A Watery Grave

Reuben should have held his breath. When the timepiece whisked him away from Skuggi, it took him to an underwater world. Reuben knew how to swim, but he didn't know how to breath underwater. And with salt water stinging his eyes, and his lungs already burning from not having enough air, he swam straight up as fast as he could. His head popped up from the surface of the ocean and he took a deep full breath of air, while treading water.

There was nothing but the rolling sea in all directions. Reuben began to think about those creatures with the red lights, their hideous faces, teeth, and tentacles. He began to think about what may have happened to the Pog who was tossed overboard.

Nope. I'm outta here.

Reuben set the timepiece for six-thirty, struggling to keep his head above the water as he did. He rubbed the timepiece but nothing happened. He popped the lid open again. The timepiece had reset itself for four o'clock.

"Oh, come on!" he screamed in frustration. Over and over again, he tried to set the watch to a different time, a different world. But the pocket watch had a mind of its own.

His arms and legs were tiring, and struggling to keep his head above water while fooling with the timepiece was becoming too difficult for him.

Tucking the watch into his right cargo pocket, he took a deep breath, and floated on his back for a while. The sky above had a purplish hue, and puffy white clouds drifted in strange shapes here and there. The water was warm, and the breeze across his nose and face was cool. Reuben's eyelids grew heavy, and while the thought of those creatures made him nervous, his body and mind were too exhausted to keep him awake...

*****

The *Spectre* sailed from Shadow Bay almost as soon as it arrived. The boys didn't have a chance to go through the shack portal, back to the orphanage, where they could rest, eat, and recover from the taxing work of plundering and battle.

Tiger, in his hurt and anger, ordered that they put to sea immediately. The result was a ship full of irritable grumpy boys. Every one of them were pouty, moody, and 'snippy'.

Except for Smitty. He watched the boys, listened to their complaints, and waited for his opportunity...

Smitty believed that a ship full of unhappy pirates could lead to 'changes in management.' The thought of being a pirate captain pleased Smitty. With a fully supplied ship, Smitty could sail freely between the the seas that bridged the worlds of the timepiece. He could skip having to risk traveling through the Chamber of Crossroads, which was heavily guarded and patrolled by the Traveler's League.

With a trained and experienced crew, he could explore the surrounding islands, and build up his force of fighting pirates. There were bound to be Trolls, Pogs, men, boys, and other creatures that would compliment his crew. And once they were big enough, *strong enough,*

Smitty would get his revenge against Toby, Hoops, and the League.

And when I get my hands on that Reuben kid... I'm going to feed him to those creatures, one little piece at a time.

*****

Reuben awoke with a jolt.

It was the sound of waves crashing on the beach that startled him. Dazed from sleeping too long, he sat up straight and tried to make sense of his surroundings. He was covered in yellow sand, and soaking wet. His clothes smelled like seaweed and fish, but he was alive.

"So you're *not* dead. That's a relief." a voice from behind him said softly.

Reuben looked behind him and saw a boy, about his age, maybe a year or two older. He had bluish green hair that hung over his ears and almost touched his shoulders. His light skin was pale and *slightly* green. He wore only a pair of canvas shorts that had been cut from some old tattered ships sails.

"I thought you might not make it. You looked dead when I found you," the boy said.

Reuben tried to remember what happened, but it was all just blank in his mind. "I was floating on the surface of the water, and I think I must have fallen asleep..."

"Floating?" the boy snickered "You weren't floating. You were sinking! You practically landed right on top of me! Scared me half to death."

"Did I drown? Am I... *dead?*" Reuben wondered aloud.

"I thought you were at first. But I drug your butt up on the beach anyway. You're the most interesting thing I've found in the ocean in a long time!"

Reuben was puzzled by the conversation, "what do you mean *I practically landed on top of you?*"

The boy grinned, his cracked lips pulling back revealing teeth that were whiter than pearls, "I was out taking my daily stroll, and something hit me in the head and fell to the sand at my feet. When I reached down to pick it up, you landed on top of me."

"I'm confused" said Reuben, "How did I get above you. I was floating on the water. Did a wave toss me onto the beach? Is that how I landed on top of you?"

"We were nowhere near the beach... we were way out there" the boy said pointing out to sea.

"My name is Albion, first born of Neptune, Prince of the Atoll, Son of the Sea, and rescuer of napping boys who appear out of nowhere." His strange grin was warm and friendly. His eyes sparkled with curiosity, and they were greener than emeralds.

"I'm Reuben, Pirate of Skuggi, also known as Dracula, and also a Traveler of

Worlds." That was the best Reuben could come up with at the moment.

The boy stood up and extended his hand, the timepiece dangled from his fingers.

"I believe this belongs to you. This is what hit me on the head out in the ocean."

"Thank you." Reuben breathed a sigh of relief as he slipped the timepiece into his pocket. "Where are we, anyway."

"We're on my island...Welcome to Isango."

The Course to Isango

The dark clouds of Skuggi finally disappeared behind them. The swells of the sea became larger and larger as a stiff forceful wind filled the *Spectre's* black sails. They were being driven faster and faster through the ocean, and the course they had set pointed them directly in the direction of the two crescent moons that hung over the horizon ahead.

The rolling and swaying of the ship, was no longer a comforting element of their voyage. It had become more of a nuisance. Crates and bottles were constantly falling over, and walking on deck required a lot of skill and balance.

Chumlick was at the helm with a depressing look on his face. Tiger Master stood beside him with a whip in his hand.

Pimple Tom was up in the crow's nest swaying this way and that way with every roll of the waves. Every once in a while, the motion would be too much for Tom, and he'd lean over and puke. The wind would carry his vomit in sheets, and sometimes a drop or two would land on Smitty, like acid rain. *Poor guy!*

But Tiger would not allow Pimple Tom to come down until he saw the Island of Isango. And if Tommy tried to leave his post, Tiger's whip would remind him of his duties.

Rat Trap was instructed to build more of his wooden cubes. Tiger ordered that he make at least a dozen more. He sat in corner working away, muttering to himself and quietly complaining.

Club Dub was scrubbing the deck with sand to make it smooth and remove any splinters. It was back breaking work and Club Dub sang out a lullaby in a whiny voice as he labored.

Smitty got down on his hands and knees and started helping Club Dub, scrubbing the deck as he quietly talked.

"Hey Clubby, don't you think the *Pogs* should be doing this work? Why is Tiger being so mean to you?"

Club Dub thought about it and made an angry, pouty face. He started scrubbing harder and harder the more he thought about it.

Smitty got up and walked over to Rat Trap and sat down. He snatched one of the cubes that had been recently finished.

"Nice work, Rat Trap. These things are amazing, by the way. Did you invent these?"

"Yeah. Thought they might come in handy... guess I was right."

Smitty smiled, "This is the coolest invention I think I've ever seen. You're a real genius! A regular Tinker Master..."

Rat Trap didn't say anything, he just kept working.

"You know, I just don't get it..." Smitty slyly suggested, "We're not going to be raiding any ships out here. The seas are too rough, and we're on a mission to sail to an island. We're not going to need any of these cubes on this voyage. Don't you think Tiger is wasting your time by having you make these right now? Surely your skills could be put to better use."

"I'm sick of this stupid ship. And Tiger up there, acting like God with a whip. He's gonna get us all killed." Rat

Trap grumbled as he kept tinkering and constructing the next cube.

Smitty patted him on the back and walked to the front of the boat. Diamond Spy stood holding the rail with shaky hands, preparing to 'toss his cookies' (puke his guts out) yet again. His dark skin looked a little pale and his eyes were getting red.

"You look terrible, Diamond!" Smitty said in the most comforting voice he could make up. "Why don't you go down and crawl into a hammock and get some rest?"

"T... t... Tiger won't l... let me. He says I'm s... s... s... supposed to keep a l... l... luh.. l..."

"Lunch bucket?" Smitty joked.

"Ugh... d... don't say l... l... lunch right now" Tiger grabbed his stomach. "I'm supposed to k... keep a l... loo... l..."

"Lobster chum?" Smitty innocently asked.

"Gah... ugh.." Diamond was on the verge of barfing. "S... st... stop it! I'm sup... supposed to keep a loo... l... l..."

"Leech mucus loaf?"

Brwaagaagaa. Diamond heaved over the side and emptied his stomach into the ocean.

"Lookout!" he shouted in anger at Smitty.

"Dang, Diamond. You really should go lay down." Smitty said, "I don't understand how you let Tiger push you around, and all."

"He's c... c... Captain."

Smitty smiled, "He may be Captain, but *you,* my friend are the magician. From what I can tell you have more power and potential than anyone on this ship... If you ask me, *you should have been Captain by now.* How did you learn your magic anyway?"

Before Diamond Spy could answer, Tiger Master shouted from the poop deck,

"Smitty! I need you on deck up here... *now* please."

The tone in Tiger Master's voice annoyed Smitty so much he clenched his teeth. *It won't be long until you regret barking orders at* me, *you piratey punk.*

"Aye-aye Cap'n." Smitty buried his irritation, and forced a smile as he bounced up the poop deck steps.

"What did you need, T-"

"Why are you whispering with my crew?" Tiger interrupted. His abrupt demanding tone caught Smitty off-guard. And before he could think to answer Tiger barked at him again, "You should be working your hands on this ship... not your mouth, you dog."

I'm gonna kill you, you little punk. Maybe not today. Maybe not this week. But I've seen your future... and it's uglier than that stupid hat you have on.

"Yes sir! I'll be happy to do whatever my Captain needs of me" Smitty said casually.

"I don't trust you. I think the other guys think you're okay, but I don't like you at all." Tiger sneered.

"But, I... *saved your life*, sir." Smitty couldn't figure this kid out. But his gratitude for being saved from Thorne had a very short life-span.

"I had everything under control I didn't need your help!" Tiger crossed his eyes and looked away.

Smitty's cheeks were bright red, his face flush with anger. His fists were balled up tightly and he grit his teeth. It was too much to handle. Smitty's pride had taken enough of the bratty pirate Captain's insults. Smitty began to step towards Tiger, his mind racing with horrid thoughts of violence.

"Land ho!" Pimple Tom shouted from the crow's nest above. "Isango, Captain! Land!"

"Where away?" Tiger called up to Tom.

"Two points off the port bow."

Tiger pulled his looking glass out and found the thin green sliver of jungle beach off in the distance ahead.

"Get down here Tom! I need you on deck." Tiger called back.

The surprise of finally spotting their destination was enough to calm Smitty and keep him from ripping Tiger Master limb from limb.

Tiger looked at the clouds above and measured the speed and force of the wind. "Put out more sail!" he ordered the pirates.

Extra spars were extended on both masts and fresh black sails were added alongside the big billowing square sails. The *Spectre* lurched forward with the wind at her back.

Tiger looked over the side of the poop deck to examine the speed of the water rushing by.

"Good! Good! We're flying now, boys!" he shouted in delight. But no one rejoiced with him. They just kept pouting and complaining to themselves.

Tiger looked at Smitty, "The chase is on, Mr. Smitty. The chase is finally on!"

Smitty looked at the island miles and miles in the distance. "What do you mean, Tiger? What are we chasing?"

"The *island* you idiot! We'll catch it this time for sure!"

The island is moving?

"Are you saying that you've never actually reached the island?"

"No. This is the closest we've ever gotten. But this time we will make it for sure! Look how fast we're sailing!"

Chumlick looked at Smitty with all hope gone from his eyes. Chumlick knew the truth. Chumlick knew that Isango would always be too far to sail to no matter how long or fast you sailed towards it. It just *never got closer.*

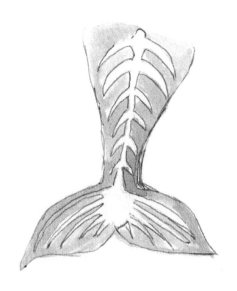

A Strange Boy

"I've been here before" Reuben said as he looked at the wall of trees, ferns and brush. The jungle was the first world the timepiece had taken him to. It was the one o'clock world. It happened only days ago, but to Reuben it felt like ancient history.

"You've been to my island? I don't remember seeing you," Albion said. "It's a pretty big island, though. And I spend all my time near the beach. I don't go very far into the jungle. I've been here for years and still don't know what's in there. Except for the *beast.*

Reuben remembered seeing a waterfall, and begin chased off by a terrible creature with long horns and orange leathery skin. "I think I may know which beast you're talking about."

Reuben and Albion sat side by side in the sand, and watched the two crescent moons setting. Reuben told Albion about his adventures. How he was given the timepiece by a tall teenager, with dark hair that swooshed over one side of his face. He told him how the timepiece was magic, and how it whisked him away to this island when he set the watch for one o'clock, how he lost his reflection in the mirror dimension, and how he discovered Shadow Bay. He told Albion about the Pirates of Skuggi, and the fight with Thorne, and about Smitty.

Albion sat staring wide-eyed at at Reuben, listening with intense curiosity.

"What will happen when you've passed through all twelve worlds of your pocket watch, I wonder?"

Reuben had wondered that himself. He felt like he was being *led* by the timepiece through these strange worlds. He felt as if there was a *purpose* to his travels.

"I don't really know. I just hope that I make it, and get back home at some point."

"Home..." Albion sighed, "I want nothing more than to go home as well."

Reuben asked, "Where's your home?"

"The sea is my home."

"But you said that you were 'taking a stroll' when you found me out there in the ocean. I don't understand. You can go into the water, but still not be home?"

Albion nodded and sighed, "I'll show you. Watch." He jumped up, grabbed Reuben's hand and pulled him to his feet.

They walked down to the water's edge and stood side-by-side.

"Stay close to me" Albion warned. He grabbed Reuben's hand and led him into the surf and waves. Reuben watched the water recoil from the presence of Albion, parting in all directions to completely avoid contact with him. Albion led them hundreds of yards away from the shore, where beautiful coral reefs surrounded them. They stood in a perfectly dry bubble of air, untouched by the water.

Reuben would have been thrilled at the beauty that surrounded him, but Albion looked so hopelessly sad that the excitement of the discovery was extinguished.

As they strolled through the twists and turns of a great reef, Albion began to share his story:

"I am the first born of Neptune. He is the King of all oceans and God of the seas. His throne is in the Atlantian Atoll, and is the source of life for all living water creatures. When I was born, my mother also gave birth to my twin sister, Cymopoleia. We grew up together exploring the vast reaches of our father's kingdoms, and pestering land walkers that dare to trespass on our ocean. It's what mermen and mermaids do by nature, you see."

Reuben interrupted, "Whoa, whoa, whoa... you mean to tell me that you're a *merman?*"

"That's right. At least, I was before the curse" Albion confessed.

"What happened?" Reuben gasped.

Albion continued:

"A long time ago, my sister and I were swimming near the shores of Sirihbaz, when a strange man beckoned us. He lured us into a small cove and there he captured my sister. His dwarven slave had built a net trap and hid it in the seaweed. The man was some kind of dark wizard, I think. I begged him to release her, but he said that he would only release her if I help him find the lair of Old Duppy. Now, my sister and I knew where Old Duppy lived. Everyone in the sea knows, and everybody avoids that terrible place. Old Duppy is a sea god, like my father, but his magic is dark and feeds on death. He collects things that fall into the sea, and most of all... he collects humans. The humans call his lair the 'locker'. It's a prison of dead and dying things.

Anyway, this wizard, Braxo was his name I think, wanted to meet Old Duppy and learn his magic. He asked that I bring Old Duppy to him within a week's time and he'd let my sister go. I swam fast and hard and found Old Duppy in his locker. I told him about my sister, and he said that he'd be happy to go meet with Braxo and help free my sister... IF... I gave him a human for his collection in return. I agreed, thinking that Braxo himself might make a fine addition to Old

Duppy's collection. When we arrived at the cove, Braxo was gone and my sister lay dead on the cove's beach, stabbed in the heart. The blade... it was still lodged in her chest."

Reuben put his hand on Albion's shoulder, "I'm so sorry."

The Son of the Sea just nodded his head, patted Reuben's hand and continued:

"Old Duppy was furious with me. I had promised him a human offering, but failed to deliver one. He went at once to my father and told him of the broken agreement. My father was enraged. He fumed at Old Duppy for his lack of sympathy. He was so angry that the water around him boiled! And my father was furious with *me* because I was foolish enough to trust a human. I went to Old Duppy when Cymo was captured, instead of going to our father for help. He blames me for her death.

"Old Duppy demanded the body of my sister for his collection. My father didn't agree at first, but according to the laws of the sea, an agreement with Old Duppy cannot be broken, or stay broken at least, without terrible consequences. My father agreed, gave Old Duppy my sister's body, and took his horrible anger out on me. He cursed me to walk on land, gave me legs in place of my tail, and lungs instead of gills. He ordered that the waters never again touch my skin, because I was no longer to be called the Son of the Sea. I was no longer to be called *his son.*"

Reuben had never heard a sadder story. He had never felt so deeply hurt for someone else as he did for Albion.

"Can the curse be broken?"

"Maybe. If I can find my sister's body, and take it back to my father, he might have mercy on me. But that would be the only way. And I'd have to make an agreement with Old Duppy, to trade a living body for a dead one."

"Albion, I think I know where to find your sister's body!" The thought flashed into his mind like lightning.

Albion's sad expression faded into curiosity.

Reuben practically shouted, "The Pirates of Skuggi have it! They have it tied to the front of their ship! It's on the *Spectre!*"

"But how can that be? It belongs to Old Duppy?"

"I don't know how, but I know what I saw on the *Spectre*. And I'm sure that it's her." Without hesitation, Reuben looked Albion directly in the eyes, put his hand on his shoulder, and proclaimed, "The Timepiece brought me here for a reason. Whether I finish my journey or not, it's obvious that I've been sent to help you. *I will help you get your sister's bones back.* The next time you see the *Spectre*, be prepared. I will cut her loose, and you can walk out into the sea with your weird bubble thing and retrieve her."

"I've given up on trusting humans. Thanks for offering, though" Albion looked away and hung his head.

"I don't care if you trust me or not. I'm going to help you. *I give you my word.*"

Albion sat on the beach with his new friend staring at the waves and the darkening purple sky. And for the first time in years, he felt *hope.*

Mutinous Dog

They sailed day and night for an entire week, but the island of Isango never got closer. Tiger Master demanded that all hands be on deck at all times. There was no time to rest. Several Pogs were lost during the race to the island. Having either fallen asleep, made a mistake in their duties, or injured themselves, Tiger Master ordered that they be tossed overboard. The killing of Pogs was nothing to the boy who captained the *Spectre.* But the crew didn't like how things were turning out.

One morning Rat Trap fell asleep while keeping watch at the front of the ship. He had been awake for two days and his exhaustion was too much to endure. When Tiger Master realized that he had dozed off, he ran to the front of the ship and whipped Rat Trap across the back several times. Dark red welts striped Rat Trap's back for several more days.

Pimple Tom accidentally dropped a bottle of black slush on the poop deck on night. Tiger was furious at the senseless waste of their provisions. He ordered Club Dub to tie Pimple Tom to the mast and give him ten lashes of the whip. Club Dub obeyed, and whipped Pimple Tom, but didn't hit as hard as he normally would have. It just wasn't as fun that time.

Club Dub accidentally fell asleep a few days later while working on the main deck. Tiger jumped on him and wailed him with his fists. He slapped his chubby cheeks several times and kicked him in the belly. Club Dub covered his head with his arms and rolled this way and that way on his back, crying and wailing. He was twice the size of Tiger Master, but he cowered under the Captain's assaults. It was Club Dub's wailing and moaning later that night, that sent the boys over the edge. Smitty could feel it.

Smitty knew the time was right. The crew was at its breaking point with Tiger Master, and the island was still in the distance far ahead of them, as if they hadn't sailed a single yard forward in weeks.

The next morning Smitty knocked on Tiger's cabin door.

"Who's there? Why aren't you working? How close is the island? Why aren't you answering me? Can't you do anything right?" Tiger shouted from behind the door.

"It's Chumlick, Captain... he fell asleep at the helm. He's steering the ship off course." Smitty lied.

Smitty heard curses and shouts coming from Tiger Master as he stumbled across the cabin and yanked the door open,

"I'm gonna skin that little toad a..." Tiger's harsh voice silenced with a *thud!* Smitty had headbutted him so hard he fell onto his back, his nose bleeding.

"How dare you!" he screamed at Smitty. But before he could get to his feet, Smitty had shut the door behind them, slipping into the cabin. He and Tiger were alone.

"Get out of my cabin!" He yelled at the redhead.

But Smitty calmly walked over to Tiger and pulled the tiger pelt hat right off of his head. "Actually, there's been a change in management. *You* are in *my* cabin, Tiger."

"Mutinous dog!" Tiger shrieked. "You're a dead man. Mutiny is punishable by death on this ship... Club Dub! In my cabin. NOW!"

A moment later, Club Dub, along with everyone except Chumlick, crowded into the Captain's cabin.

"Take Smitty below and clap him in irons! And get a long rope. We're going to hang him for mutiny!" Tiger was on his feet wiping blood from his face on his shirt sleeve.

Smitty turned to the boys, looking each one in the eye, and said "I have a better idea. How about Tiger Master shut his big mouth, and let somebody else be the Captain for a while; somebody who won't beat you, or slap you, or whip you. Someone who won't work you to death, then punish you for dying. Someone who won't toss a perfectly good living creature overboard like trash. Someone who realized that we're chasing an *unreachable* island and won't get us all killed.

The boys were shouting and grunting in agreement with Smitty. Tiger Master's eyes began to widen with fear.

Smitty turned around and stared at Tiger as Diamond Spy's voice suddenly filled the room, "I.. s... ssss... say that we take a v... v... v... vote on it."

The boys all agreed.

"I don't care who you vote for captain so long as it's *not* this freckled-face brat!" Smitty lied. "All in favor of Tiger Master continuing as Captain, raise your hand."

Only one hand shot up, and it was Tiger's. "Come on, guys! I've been with you for years. I've wiped your noses, cleaned up your messes, and gotten you out of trouble hundreds of times."

No one said a word.

Diamond Spy broke the silence, "All in f... f... favor of Smitty as C... C... Ca... C..."

"...*Captain*, raise your hands." Rat Trap interrupted.

Everyone's hand went up except for two, Tiger's... and Smitty's.

Smitty looked around the room and sighed, "Well, it looks like this is my cabin after all!" he laughed.

"My first order as Captain is that we clap Tiger in irons for the rest of the journey back to Shadow Bay. I'll tell Chumlick to turn the ship around right now."

The boys cheered as Smitty pushed past them and bounced up the steps to the poop deck. He tossed the tiger pelt hat into the ocean, then turned to Chumlick.

"Turn the ship around Chumlick. We're going home. Chumlick?... Chumlick?"

The prim and proper pirate lay slumped over the wheel of the ship. He *had* fallen asleep after all.

The Crystal Queen

The Crystal Queen sat on her throne listening to two WolliPogs squabble over the ownership of a tiny farm near the WolliPog village. She had listened to many such arguments since returning from the six-thirty world with her people.

When her world had been freed from the darkness of Petros O' Magos, and his shadow wizards, there was much to rebuild. Food needed to be grown, villages rebuilt, and Castle Mavros (which had been almost completely gutted by fire) had to be restored.

Her first official decree as Queen was that all WolliPogs in Sirihbaz or any other world were *free people.* This won her the love and admiration of the race, and the entire world of Sirihbaz.

As the two WolliPogs waved their hands and shouted at each other, GeriPog burst into the throne chamber and rushed across the stone floor. When he reached the foot of Queen Mae's throne, he bowed deeply and said, "I have very urgent news, my queen."

"What is it, Lord GeriPog?"

"A visitor has come. A boy named Reuben. He carries the *timepiece.*"

Queen Mae lept from her throne in excitement.

"A Traveler! How wonderful! Where is he? I want to greet him immediately."

"He's at our gates, majesty. I'll show him in now."

The silver bearded dwarf disappeared momentarily. When he returned to the Queen's throne chamber he was followed by a tall boy with light brown hair. His face was red from sunburn, revealing small brown freckles on his cheeks. His eyes were light blue, like crystals, and when he looked at her, she thought they were striking.

Reuben stood in the middle of her chamber and told his story; how he discovered Shadow Bay, and the *Spectre*. He told her about the Pirates of Skuggi and the battle with Thorne.

Queen Mae said, "Diambi won't be happy when she hears about Thorne's death. But we must tell her... GeriPog, I'll need you to travel to Hapis."

"I will, my queen."

Reuben continued to tell about Tiger Master's treatment of the WolliPog slaves, and how he traded them with Marsh

Trolls and King Boglack. He told her about the whippings, and Pogs being tossed overboard, and made to walk the plank.

Queen Mae wiped tiny tears from her eyes and said, "GeriPog, I'll need you to set a patrol along the coast to watch for the pirates. We also need to prepare a fighting force to stop them. They'll kidnap no more WolliPogs from my kingdom."

" I will my queen"

When Reuben told Queen Eva Mae about the redheaded prisoner named 'Smitty' she jumped to her feet and cried, "No! It can't be! He's back?"

GeriPog grumbled, "Not to worry, my queen. I trapped the Fox once before, and I can do it again. He has no shadow wizards or dragons with him this time."

Queen Mae nodded her head, "True, but we still have to be careful. And if we catch him, we can't kill him. Toby has unsettled business with him. Let the League deal with Smitty. We'll deal with the pirates. GeriPog, will you go to Traveler's Rest to inform them of this news?"

"I will my queen" GeriPog grumbled again, "but if I may... what in the world should I do first? Go to Hapis, set a patrol along the coasts, train a fighting force, set a trap for the Fox, or go to Traveler's Rest?"

The Crystal Queen realized that she was asking too much of her most trusted friend and said, "Right. Sorry GeriPog."

"Your majesty, that's not the entire story. There is something else. On Isango, there is a boy named Albion..." Reuben told her the incredibly sad story of Neptune's son, and his curse. "He's my friend. The only true friend I've found on this weird journey. And I made a promise to help him break his curse, but I need help. I don't think I can do it alone."

Queen Mae instructed GeriPog to go to Traveler's Rest first, and then told Reuben that she wanted to help but she first needed to make sure her people, the WolliPogs were safe.

"I'm afraid I can't help much right now... but maybe the Traveler's League can. We'll ask Toby when he arrives."

Reuben smiled at her and bowed in gratitude.

Queen Mae felt a strange flutter when he bowed. There was something different about Reuben. He spoke softly and was quiet. But he cared deeply about the WolliPogs, and his friend Albion. His eyes sparkled when he talked about them. And when he looked at the Crystal Queen, she couldn't keep from blushing.

Old Duppy

"So there's this group of New Town brats that call themselves the *Traveler's League.*" Smitty leaned on the rail of the poop deck. He was watching Isango drift away behind them. Diamond Spy was at the helm and had asked about the timepiece. All the other pirates were below decks, sleeping in their hammocks.

"They have this timepiece that transports them from world to world. When a boy is first given the pocket watch, he must travel to each world at least once. If he makes it through all twelve worlds, he becomes a member of their little do-gooder club."

"How does it w... w... work?" Diamond asked. "Is their a s...s... sp... spell or s... something?"

Smitty shook his head. "Nah. You just set the hands of the pocket watch to the hour that represents the world you want to go to. Anyone can do it."

Diamond Spy had been very curious about the magic of the timepiece. When Reuben had disappeared right before his eyes, he realized that there was more magic out there for him to learn. And an item that allowed one to travel easily between twelve different worlds seemed to be worth more than all the gold and black slush in the world to Diamond.

"Since we're talking about magic" Smitty smiled, "you never answered my question. How did you learn *your* magic."

"W... what m... m... mm....magic? I only know a c...c...couple of t...tr... tricks." Diamond said as casually as a stuttering boy could.

Smitty said, "A couple of tricks? Come on, Diamond. I know what I saw when we went through that whirlpool portal thingy."

"W... w... w... wormpools. We c... c... call 'em wormpools."

"Wormpools. Right. And from what I can figure, *you* are the key to open them." Smitty took the helm and motioned for Diamond to take his turn resting on the rail. "I heard you chanting in a strange language. And the ocean seemed to obey. And your eyes.... I saw them. They were glowing bright blue! At first I thought it was just the crystal in your staff. But right before we went through the wormpool, I opened my eyes and looked at you. Your eyes were blazing like blue stars."

Diamond didn't say anything. He just looked down at the deck.

"You're no orphan from Old Town" Smitty continued. "I don't even think that you're from my world at all. So you can stop pretending." Smitty's accusation was met with silence, but he kept talking. "Look, all the other pirates assume that your staff and your hat are magical items. They think that those *things*, those possessions, are special. But I know that's not true. I know the magic is inside *you*, somehow; not your hat or your staff. That's what makes you different from the other pirates... Who are you *really?*"

Diamond looked at Smitty and gave a big white toothy grin, the first Smitty had seen from the dark-skinned boy. "Y... you're on to me, S... Sm... Smitty. I'm not l... l... like you g... guys."

"What's your *real* name?" Smitty asked a little nervously.

Diamond smiled, stood up and raised his hands in the air, stretching them out over the water. He clapped his palms together three times. *Slap, slap, slap.*

The sky immediately darkened and a black cloud formed above the ship. The waters around the *Spectre* became choppy. Smitty heard slapping splashing sounds all around the boat. He looked over the rail and saw thousands of red lights glowing in the dark waters.

Diamond's eyes were once again glowing like bright blue orbs, powered by some strange magical force within the tall dark-skinned boy. He gazed at Smitty, who was holding on the to rail with both hands, frozen with fear.

Without stuttering, he opened his mouth and a deep voice that sounded like a rumble bubbling up through a snorkel tube came out of Diamond's mouth.

"I'm known in many worlds." Diamond said without stuttering, then he began to sing and chant:

> "The lost, the drifting,
> the offerings that float.
> The sailor that falls,
> the fast sinking boat.
> I keep them, collect them.
> I eat them, resurrect them.
> I am the god of the wave,
> and god of the grave.
> The wave is the grave."

Smitty fell to his knees in fright, shielding his eyes from the terrible being before him. Diamond raised his voice again, filling the air with a thundering chant:

> "I am older than land,
> and stronger than the sea.
> All that swim and die,
> belong to me."

The Oracle

"Welcome, young traveler" the gentle voice flowed up from the darkness of the well.

"Are you the Oracle?" *Dumb question. Of course this is the Oracle,* Reuben thought as soon as the words left his mouth.

"Dumb question, Reuben. Of course I'm the Oracle" the voice teased.

"Right. That makes sense I guess. I'm Reuben." *Idiot. The Oracle knows your name. It just said 'Reuben'.*

"I know, you silly boy. I just used your name didn't I?" the voice answered back. "And you're not an idiot."

Reuben took a breath and calmed himself before he continued. The little stone wishing well waited quietly as he did, with only a cool breeze flowing up from it's dark hole. The breeze smelled familiar, like fish and seaweed, but it was mixed with something sweet like caramel and mint.

The Oracle spoke before Reuben had his thoughts together, "The Crystal Queen has sent you to me, yes?"

"That's right. Queen Mae said that I needed to ask you for help."

"Ah... the *Queen Mae*. The prophecy was fulfilled, then. She defeated Braxo and is restoring Sirihbaz. Good."

Reuben was unsure of what all of that meant. He only wanted to learn how to help his friend Albion.

"Oracle, I need your help."

"You want to know how to free the Son of Neptune from his curse..."

"Exactly!" Reuben exclaimed. "How can I help my friend?"

"The deal with Old Duppy, Duffer, the collector of death, has been made. The die cast. You cannot take the princess's body from him without offering a living body in return. It is the ancient law of the sea."

"And what happens if I do it anyway? What happens if I break this *ancient law of the sea?*" Reuben asked angrily.

"The oceans of the four gates and five worlds will flood. The lands will disappear, and all life will slowly drown, unless the balance is restored. If the law remains broken, the worlds and all living things, will die a watery death."

"Yikes. That stinks." Reuben thought for a moment. "If I make the trade with Old Duppy, and help Albion return his sister's body to Neptune, will his father remove the curse?"

"That is for Neptune to decide... but you cannot make the trade." The Oracle said softly.

"What?!"

"You cannot give what you do not have."

"What do you mean?!" Reuben shouted in confused frustration.

The ground shook. The pebbles at Reuben's feet bounced around his toes. He grabbed the edge of the well to steady himself, and after about ten seconds of rumbling, the quake stopped.

"You cannot save your friend" the Oracle said. "Only the Black Fox can save Albion."

"Who's the Black Fox?" Reuben asked nervously.

The ground shook again, this time the rumbling was more violent.

"It's time for you to leave, Reuben. I have given you your answers."

"But where should I go? How do I help Albion? Should I finish my travels, first? Will the League help me?" Reuben's voice bounced from his mouth as the ground started shaking more violently.

"Use the timepiece, Reuben" the Oracle wailed, "find the Black Fox. And don't break the agreement with Old Duppy... Only the Black Fox can save your friend."

Reuben pulled the timepiece from his pocket. This was not the answer he had come for. The Oracle did not seem as helpful the Crystal Queen had led him to believe.

I'll just have save Albion myself he thought as he set the timepiece for one o'clock again.

But the pocket watch reset itself to eight o'clock as Reuben was caught up in the glowing tornado of magic dust.

Whoosh.

A Wild Shore

The magic of the timepiece slowed and cleared away from Reuben's sight. An icy wave of water rushed up around him, splashed his chest, and covered his face. Cold salty water ran up his nose and stung his eyes. He scrambled backwards, crab walking backwards up the beach.

His hands and feet pushing away rough pebbles and shells embedded in the coarse dark sand. Another wave rushed towards him but he was far enough up the beach to avoid it. At his back was the edge of a dark pine forest that thickened as it stretched away from the rugged unwelcoming beach.

It must have been morning because the air was rushing over the tree tops and out to sea. Reuben remembered reading somewhere about how the wind comes off the water at night, and changes direction in the morning. Also, way out in the dark grey waters of the ocean, a thin strip of orange light traced the horizon. Reuben stared at the glowing line as is got thicker, wider, and more brilliant as the sun rose from behind the forest at his back.

It was a glorious sight. And the smell of pine and salt complimented the stunning seascape that Reuben believed only God could paint so beautifully.

For few brief minutes, he had forgotten how he'd gotten there, where he had come from, and what his mission was. His mind took a break as he breathed in the pinewood beach and listened to the chirping of gulls and squirrels.

As the sun continued to rise, a sharp sparkle of light glinted on the edge of the horizon. Something out there in the ocean was moving and reflecting the sun's beam. The object turned and the reflection blinked off, leaving a dark grey dot floating miles away from the beach. Reuben knew right away that it wasn't an animal. The slow bulky glide across the water could only be made by a ship. And it was a large one!

Reuben jumped back on the beach and ran to the water's edge waving his arms above his head wildly, yelling as loud as he could.

"Hello! Help! You there! Over here!"

The ship continued to glide across the sea, but it got slightly larger as it came nearer to the shore.

"Here! Over here! Help! Hello there! Over he..." Reuben froze when he saw the familiar grey wood of the ship's hull and the black sails billowing full of ocean wind.

It was the *Spectre!*

The ship was heading directly for the beach and Reuben feared that Smitty had spotted him through his looking glass. Or perhaps Pimple Tom has seen him from his perch in the crow's nest. Reuben ran back into the forest and hid behind a large pine as he watched the *Spectre* make its way towards him. He pulled the timepiece from his pocket and checked the hour... eight o'clock!

Again? This timepiece takes me wherever it wants. I don't know why I even bother setting it at all. I must be here for a reason.

Reuben stayed hidden in the forest and watched as the *Spectre* anchored about a hundred hundreds yards from the shore line. Two small dinghies (row boats) were lowered and several kid pirates piled into each. They rowed straight for the beach and rode the breaking waves up to the rocky sand.

Smitty and Pimple Tom were the tallest of all the boys. Smitty was dressed in black from head to toe. He jumped out of his dinghy and began ordering the other boys to remove the boxes and chests and bring them up to the edge of the wood. Rat Trap and Club Dub were there as well, quietly following orders. But Reuben didn't recognize any of the other boys. There were new faces... a lot of them! Most of them were young. Reuben guessed that they were eight and nine year olds. And when Reuben slipped behind a closer tree to get a better look, he noticed that there were even girls in this new crew!

Smitty softly ordered the new girls to start setting up camp on the beach while he and the new boys prepared to bury their treasure. Reuben was close enough to make out what Smitty was saying.

"Pimple Tom! I need you to stay here with the newbies and make sure camp gets set up. It's gonna be cold tonight and we'll need a good strong fire. There's some black slush in those crates over there if you guys get thirsty."

Pimple Tom smiled and nodded "Awright, Cap'n. And what about *hee'im?*" Tom pointed to one boy still sitting in a dinghy with his hands tied behind his back, and his mouth gagged. His face was freckled and his messy hair was reddish brown. He had familiar piercing blue eyes and a snotty nose that pointed upwards.

Tiger Master! Reuben realized that Smitty had mutinied and taken over as Captain. But he didn't really feel sorry for Tiger. Smitty seemed nicer. And he was a better fighter, and a much better leader, even though he was extremely dangerous.

"Bring him over by the fire and keep a close eye on him. I don't want any surprises. Don't let any of the newbies to talk to him, either." Smitty held up a shovel and looked at it thoughtfully as he said, "When we ship out in the morning, I'll take care of Tiger once and for all."

The Camp

Reuben's stomach growled. He felt as if he hadn't eaten in days. Eventually his hunger was stronger than his fear of getting caught. So when Smitty, Rat Trap, Club Dub and a group of boys disappeared into the forest to bury their treasure, Reuben decided to sneak into the camp and steal some black slush.

The new girls sat around the fire talking and giggling as Pimple Tom flexed his scrawny sunburnt arms. There weren't many muscles to show off but he liked the sound of girls laughing and giggling so he entertained them with his skeleton-like physique.

Tiger was sitting just outside the ring of pirates with his face to the fire and his back to the woods. Reuben noticed his hands fidgeting behind his back, digging through the pebbles and broken shells while no one was looking.

Reuben stayed in the shadows and crawled onto the beach and behind the crates where the black slush was stored. When the girls all laughed at Pimple Tom again, he slowly lifted the lid and pulled out a black leather bottle. He could tell from how heavy it was that it was full. His stomach growled again so loudly that he thought someone would hear. But Pimple Tom and the pirate girls were too preoccupied to hear anything above their own laughter.

Reuben stealthily crawled back into the forest and hid behind a tree. He popped the cork out and took a long slow drink. The warm black liquid was sugary and thick, filling his stomach and making his head feel light. It was like drinking maple syrup and pancakes! There was a smoky flavor to it, kind of like bacon, and it only took of a couple of swigs before Reuben started feeling... different. It was an amazing sensation. He felt hopeful, brave, and calm. *No wonder they love this stuff so much!*

Reuben peeked around the tree and listened to Pimple Tom bragging to the group of pirate girls.

"Ya'll should'a seen it! Grown men was droppin' like flies right and left. Diamond used his magic to turn one of Thorne's men into a puddle of water, and the Black Fox beat the livin' daylights out of their Cap'n with his bare hands."

The Black Fox? Reuben was stunned. That was the name the Oracle had mentioned. That was the only person who could save his friend Albion.

"Later on" Tom continued, "it was the Black Fox who took over and saved us all from dyin' at sea. Walked right into Tiger's cabin, head-butted him, and took over as Cap'n. We didn't argue. We was glad that someone new was takin' over."

Oh my gosh! Smitty is the Black Fox!

Reuben's head was swimming. How in the world was he supposed to convince Smitty to help his friend? He had basically promised the redhead that they would use the timepiece together and escape, but Reuben left him behind and traveled on to Sirihbaz alone.

I should have kept my word. Dang it.

Reuben peeked around the tree again watched the circle of pirate girls and Pimple Tom. They were passing around a bottle of black slush and enjoying themselves by the fire. But something was off. Something didn't look the same. Reuben examined the setting more closely looking at each face glowing from the red flame of the fire pit. One by one he counted them all before realizing that Tiger Master was nowhere to be found!

Hunting The Tiger

When Smitty and the boys came back to camp, Pimple Tom was standing next to the pile of supply crates. He was waving a makeshift torch this way and that way, peering into the darkness. Half of the girls were sent back to the dinghies with torches as well, while the other half stood watch around the fire.

"What in the world are you doing, Tom?" Smitty asked as he stomped over to the warmth of the fire.

"Tiger got away."

Smitty spun around looking to where he had left Tiger Master bound and gagged near the fire. A piece of cut rope lay on the pebble beach, with a sharp broken shell next to it.

Pimple Tom could feel Smitty's anger boiling inside him. All the pirates could. Everyone held their breath expecting the Black Fox to explode in rage. Tom was shaking in fear, knowing that he would be the object of the Captain's violence.

The beach was silent and all eyes were on Smitty.

The redheaded Captain took a deep breath through his nostrils, put both fists on his hips, and turned to look at Pimple Tom.

"For someone whose main job is to be the ship's lookout, you sure are terrible at it."

Pimple Tom looked down at his feet in shame and said nothing.

A big smile split across Smitty's face and he began laughing, "Don't worry about it Tom. I was going to cut him loose when we left tomorrow anyway. He'd die if I left him here all tied up. I just wanted to teach him a lesson."

Every pirate, boys and girls alike, breathed a sigh of relief… especially Tom.

"Rat Trap and Club Dub took me to where Tiger had all the treasure hidden. We moved it to a new spot and buried it with all our recent treasure" Smitty said with an air of pride. "Tiger will never find it. And by the time we get back, I'm sure his blood will have cooled down and he'll be ready to join back up with us."

"You're gonna let him come back?" Tom's brows furrowed over his sharp eyes.

"I need every skilled pirate I can get. And besides, if he goes back to that orphanage of yours, he could block up the portal and trap you guys here. I hate him, for sure. But we need him on our side." Smitty looked around and formulated a plan. "Tom, you may have let him get away, but you did well to have the girls watch the dinghies while you guarded the camp. I still want to stay the night on the beach. It's cramped on the *Spectre* and these newbies need a break... We'll ship out in the morning."

*****

Reuben lay in the dark behind his pine tree. The camp was in full view, and Smitty's fire looked so warm he wondered if being a warm captive was better than a free spy. He tried to sleep, but sleep wouldn't come. For one, it was way too chilly. Two, the ground was lumpy and hard. And three, Tiger was somewhere in the dark woods, hiding, waiting, and possibly planning some mischief.

Hours went by and all the pirates were curled up on the beach next to the fire. Each had a thick blanket that made Reuben jealous. The boys and girls that had been chosen to take shifts watching the camp while the others slept eventually fell asleep as well.

As dawn approached, the cold had sunk down so deep into Reuben that his violent shivers made his whole body ache. He knew he was here to convince Smitty to help him, and it no longer made sense to remain hidden. His fear of being thrashed by Smitty for his betrayal waned. And his need for warmth took over his thoughts and will.

Reuben stood to his feet and walked towards the edge of the wood. But just before he stepped out from behind a tree and onto the beach, he saw movement in the corner of his eye. He froze and stared into the darkness to his left. A tall shadow tiptoed onto the beach towards the camp.

It was Tiger Master, sneaking into the camp. Reuben knew that he was up to no good, but didn't know what to do. So he watched.

Tiger stayed in the shadows, and carefully walked around the entire camp. He circled all the sleeping boys and girls near the fire and stopped near where Smitty lay. The Captain was sound asleep with his bright red hair and his face poking out from under his blanket. He was sound asleep and his back was to the shadows, where Tiger was slowly and treacherously creeping towards him.

Reuben saw something metal in Tiger's hand. The light of the fire reflected off of the steel spade of a shovel. His heart began racing as he knew that Tiger would use the shovel to murder the Captain in his sleep.

The words of the Oracle echoed through his half frozen brain, *Only the Black Fox can save Albion.* Reuben panicked as he had no weapons, and there were no rocks he could throw. Tiger crept up and was now standing directly above Smitty, with the shovel in both hands.

Reuben ran out of the woods. He tried to shout but the words got stuck in his throat. The horror of what Tiger was about to do had gripped him and his body moved uncontrollably. Tiger raised the shovel above his head ready to strike the spade down onto the sleeping Captain. The campfire lit his freckled bratty face, and Reuben saw murder in Tiger's eyes, a wild evil anger, with a touch of crazed delight.

Without thinking, Reuben grabbed the only heavy thing his hands could find, the timepiece. As he struggled to yank it from his pocket he activated the magic within accidentally. He turned sideways, skipped, and hurled the pocket watch, screaming with all his might.

Magic sparkles trailed the watch as it soared through the air like a comet.

Smitty's eyes opened at the sound of Reuben's scream and he sat straight up in surprise. He watched as the timepiece arched over the fire, and struck Tiger Master in the forehead.

The pocket watch vanished the moment it slammed into the boy's forehead…

And so did Tiger Master.

The End

(Turn the page for a sample chapter of
The Traveler's League ~ Book 5: The Black Fox)

The Black Fox

Book 5 of the Traveler's League

By Nick Goss

The Spectre

"Land ho!" the cry sounded from above.

Smitty could hear it from his cabin. But it was the thumping of feet on the deck above his cabin that shook him from his daydream.

It was a great dream, and exciting as it was to spot land after weeks at sea, he preferred to stay in the dream. He desperately tried to recreate the fantasy. He closed his eyes and reconstructed the scene: a wooden club house filled with long pub-style tables and benches, crates and boxes everywhere, and a big yellow curtain with "TL" embroidered in giant bright red letters. There were people in this daydream too; Eli, his spectacled friend to whom he owed the deepest apology. There was Hoops, the newest recruit who defeated the Squid Shark, tricked the Minotaur, and broke the Old Rule.

Most of all, there was Toby; the dark haired teen, only a year older than Smitty. Toby, who beat Smitty in their weekly chess games... *everytime*. Toby, the expert Timepiece retriever and most experienced Traveler. Toby, who was voted the new Captain of the Traveler's League after Smitty bitterly betrayed his post and clubmates. Toby, who had always been Smitty's best friend, until the betrayal.

The daydream warmed Smitty's heart as he recounted all the wonderful memories before everything went to rubbish.

And it was his fault.

He ruined everything when his pride got the better of him. The memory of his betrayal of the Traveler's League shattered his dream like the popping of a balloon over and over again.

"My good Captain? May I enter?" Chumlick's muffled prim and proper voice floated through the gray wooden doors of the cabin.

Smitty wanted solitude. He wanted to stay in his cabin and swim in his memories.

But his crew needed him. They needed his leadership, and his protection. They needed what the crew of orphans could never find back in the six-thirty world. They needed a big brother, a parent, a caregiver that understood their hearts and desires. They needed someone strong and kind.

Smitty didn't see himself as the perfect fit to lead these misfit children anymore, but he was the only one who could keep them safe.

With the pain of his past still aching in his stomach, he made a silent promise to himself to never again fail those who followed him. *Never again!*

"Enter."

The cabin door creaked open and Chumlick hurried in, shuffling his spectacles on his nose and closing the door behind him. He was called the 'prim and proper pirate.' He was the youngest of the crew, raised in a wealthy family, and always neatly dressed, and overly mannered, if not polite. With a smart salute to Smitty (touching the knuckle of the forefinger to his right brow) he informed the captain.

"It is with great relief and pleasure" Chumlick recited in his best fake British accent, "that the coast of our destination Sirihbaz has been spotted."

"Are we sure it's Sirihbaz, helmsman?" Smitty straightened his back, lifting his red head from his hands. He sat at his cabin table, with maps, quills, and an inkwell all positioned haphazardly.

"Aye, Captain Fox. Pimple Tom spotted it from the mainmast crow's nest, and confirmed seeing the sparkling glint of Castle Mavros' tallest tower."

"Smitty" the Captain replied.

Chumlick raised a single eyebrow over his round spectacle frames, "Beg pardon, sir?"

"You called me 'Captain Fox'. I don't like that. I'd prefer you just call me 'Smitty.' I am the *Black Fox*, sure. And to my crew, I like to be known as 'captain'. My friends should address me as just 'Smitty.'"

Chumlick looked away in surprise, a small smile curling on the sides of his mouth.

"Very well, sir... uh... Smitty. What are your orders for the crew?"

"We'll head west along the coast and anchor at the mouth of the river." Smitty rose from his chair and put his hands on his hips, which was his way of giving orders, "and have Reuben sent to my cabin at once, please."

"Aye, aye... Cap.... er Smitty." Chumlick replied with another perfectly rehearsed salute.

Smitty could see the young boy smiling to himself as he hurried out of the Captain's cabin. *No need to be on a power trip.*

As the door clicked shut, a loud commotion rang out from the main deck. Boys were whooping and hollering, shouting and cheering. Smitty didn't mind the noise until he heard the clinking and clashing of steel against steel. His heart beat just a little faster as he hurried to the door, his mind rolling through all the possible reasons for swords to be crossed. *Are we under attack? No. We would have spotted a ship approaching. Perhaps a mutiny? That can't be. These kids look up to me like I'm their babysitter.*

Smitty rushed out onto the deck with his own sword in his hand, but still in the sheath.

The sight was both surprising and comical. Reuben, the timid Traveler, was crossing swords with RatTrap, an experienced fighter. And while Reuben was considerably taller, RatTrap had been in a hundred battles, and knew how to swing a sword. Reuben had barely escaped getting his head chopped off a while back when the ship was attacked by Queen Diambi's sailor-soldiers. That was Reuben's first battle. It was almost his last, too.

Smitty said nothing to stop the fight, as there was no tension rippling through the crowd of kids. There didn't seem to be any anger between the two boys fighting. RatTrap was laughing, actually. Reuben was scowling in frustration as he tripped over his own feet.

Whack!

The flat edge of RatTrap's blade smacked Reuben in the arm.

"Ouch!"

"Your parry was too slow. You gotta keep your wrist higher..." RatTrap offered, his brown eyes glowing with delight.

Smitty continued to watch Reuben clumsily deflect (sometimes) the blows from RatTrap's sword. Beads of sweat trickled down Reuben's face and neck, his chest red from sunburn. Dark pink lines criss-crossed each other all over his arms, belly, and back; the marks of an education hard-won.

Reuben wore a bright red bandana on his head, with only a few locks of straight brown hair poking out over his ears.

Smitty belted out, "You are actually starting to look like a pirate, Dracula!" That was Reuben's nickname, given to him by the former captain, as Reuben had no shadow. He lost it when he began his travels with the Timepiece, and never figured out how to retrieve it. And since vampires have no shadow, it was a perfect nickname for the new kid on the ship.

When Reuben heard Smitty's voice among the cheers and laughs of the onlookers, he turned his head.

Whack!

A fresh blow to the back of the head sent Reuben tumbling to the deck. He fell to his hands and knees right in front of Smitty's black boots.

"That's enough, RatTrap" the Captain sternly warned, "No more lessons today."

RatTrap grinned ear-to-ear, "Aye-aye Cap. He's taken enough *education* today I guess."

Reuben rose to his feet, rubbing the bump on his head and holding back tears.

Smitty patted him on the shoulder, "You'll be alright. I'm just glad to see you training! Come into my cabin. I need to talk to you about something."

Chumlick quickly dispersed the crowd of orphan pirates. Captain Smitty's orders were called out and the crew began pulling ropes to adjust the sails, while Chumlick steered the *Spectre* westward along the coast of Sirihbaz towards the mouth of the Forgotten River.

... to be continued!

Made in the USA
Coppell, TX
02 November 2020